DEAD RECKONINGS

A Review of Horror and the Weird in the Arts
Edited by Alex Houstoun and Michael J. Abolafia

No. 35 (Spring 2024)

DEAD RECKONINGS is published by Hippocampus Press, P.O. Box 641, New York, NY 10156 (www.hippocampuspress.com). Copyright © 2024 by Hippocampus Press. Cover art by Jason C. Eckhardt. Cover design by Barbara Briggs Silbert. Hippocampus Press logo by Anastasia Damianakos. Orders and subscriptions should be sent to Hippocampus Press. Contact Alex Houstoun at deadreckoningsjournal@gmail.com for assignments or before submitting a publication for review.

ISSN 1935-6110   ISBN 9781614984467

Evenson Collection Well Worth Reading

Tony Fonseca

BRIAN EVENSON. *None of You Shall Be Spared*. Central Point, OR: Weird House Press/Gallows Whisper, 2023. 286 pp. $19.95 tpb. ISBN: 9781957121659.

Brian Evenson's short story collection *Song for the Unraveling of the World* (2019) won the Shirley Jackson Award and the World Fantasy Award, and it was a finalist for the *Los Angeles Times'* Ray Bradbury Prize for Science Fiction, Fantasy, and Speculative Fiction. His previous works have won the International Horror Guild Award and have been finalists for the Edgar Award. He has won three O. Henry Prizes, an NEA fellowship, and a Guggenheim Award. As you can imagine, a new collection by Evenson, particularly one dedicated to the brilliant Peter Straub, is somewhat of an event to be celebrated.

Indeed, that is the case for most of the twenty-one stories (one being a novella) in *None of You Shall Be Spared*, which are as expertly written as any that I have had the pleasure of reading, by anyone. Evenson is quite the wordsmith, so fans of masterfully written sentences and evocative imagery will be quite pleased with this collection. The problem I had, and this is more about my personal taste than it is about the writing, is that some stories are underdeveloped; once I was finished reading them, I had no idea what happened, why it happened, or what the point was. It is very difficult to invest emotionally in a story if you're not sure what it is that you have read once you're finished. Granted, this is explained in the Story Notes that Evenson supplies at the end of the book: many of these stories were commissioned for anthologies whose editors were very specific in what they wanted thematically and stylistically. Nonetheless, this otherwise brilliant collection is marred by their inclusion. But I can safely say that reading *None of You Shall Be Spared* will be a worthwhile experience for fans of erudite and imaginative horror.

Part of that experience is the Story Notes section itself, which is enlightening for readers who want to get more from each of the stories. The notes are often filled with interesting glimpses into the mind of Evenson himself. He begins them by writing that "For a long time, I was reluctant to write story notes: it felt to me on the one hand a bit like revealing a little too specifically how the sausage was made and, on the other hand, like lying about how the sausage was made, making up a fable about how the story came to be." Noting that story notes are not significantly different from answering questions at readings, Evenson warms himself to the idea:

> Is it a true account? Yes, mostly. Or true enough anyway. Am I forgetting things that were important? No doubt. Am I leaving out things that may not make sense if you haven't been living inside of my head? Definitely. Are there things that were probably important subconsciously that I'm simply not aware of? Yes, probably. If you asked me on another day would other things come up? Undoubtedly.

Given the wisdom of these words, which all writers would probably agree hit the mark, Evenson further suggests words of wisdom for readers as well: read the stories first, using the notes later as a way to gain a better appreciation for them. Fortunately, I followed his advice, and I believe that my reading experience was better for it.

As mentioned, the collection does contain some masterful stories. These include the opening tale, "Knock, Knock," as well as "The Train's Path," "Stricken," "Dominion," "Lost Dog," "A Bloody Hand to Shake," and "The Fourth Scene." Others that are masterful in their wordsmithery but are slightly (only slightly) weakened by either their vagueness of detail or their non-endings are "In the Nursery," "Waiting for Mother," "Homecoming," and the novella that ends the collection, "Baby Leg." The collection does include weak contributions, some of which come across as space fillers. These include tales that are simply not horror, "Gyr" and "And Yet," and tales that seem more like dream visions than anything else, or perhaps parts of a story that need to be joined with the rest of the story, such as "I Cannot Remember," "Whet," and

"Leaving Leeds." "Whet" is, thankfully, the collection's only example of flash fiction, which, while being a great exercise or springboard, rarely (to me at least) results in an actual story.

A candidate for the best story in the collection (along with "Stricken" and "Dominion"), "Knock, Knock" was written, according to Evenson, for an Ellen Datlow–edited anthology titled *Screams from the Dark: Tales of Monsters and the Monstrous*. It was based on two ideas: a bloated body and one of Clark Ashton Smith's sculptured heads. Its main character, Hakon (the name is Scandinavian for "chosen son"), is indeed chosen, as a potential host for his father's spirit after his death. What makes the story work wonderfully are the subtle clues that are intended to establish the supernatural quality of the story. The plot is simple. Hakon's father has pit him against his uncle. The father, who was known in life as being someone who liked to create tension and push people's buttons, individually leaves his house and land to both Hakon and the uncle, thus causing them to argue. As the father expected, Hakon kills his uncle, thus providing his father with the originally intended host body; however, Hakon disposes of the body in a pond, causing damage. The uncle returns, and the first supernatural clue is given when he cannot enter the home until Hakon invites him. With a now useless body, Hakon's father's spirit attempts to kill Hakon, who ends up setting the house on fire to escape. The story ends with an eerie standoff—Hakon standing inside the burned husk of the house while the undead creature (still in the body of the uncle and now much faster than before) stands just outside the burned door frame, waiting to be invited in. This may well be one of the best horror story endings I have ever read.

"The Train's Path" is a fascinating tale about a boy who sees his friend David killed as he gets dragged by a train for a mile (the boys had been placing pennies on the track, and David slipped when trying to run away from the train, which caught his pant leg). Its central premise is that witnessing this event has opened the unnamed narrator's mind so that he is now able to see the ghost bodies of living people when they undergo some kind of trauma (or he perceives that they have). It also gives him a fear of trains and tracks, so he stays away from both. The story ends with his being enraptured by a painting in the National Gallery, until he realizes that in the background is an oncoming train, which runs over his ghost body; his ghost body remains there, in front of the painting. He returns often just to view it. According to Evenson's notes, "The Train's Path" was envisioned when Alcebiades Diniz Miguel asked for a contribution for an anthology titled *Ghost, Speed and the Machine*, based on J. M. W. Turner's 1844 painting *Rain, Steam, and Speed—The Great Western Railway*. It is also inspired by the Lumière Brothers' 1896 film *Arrival of a Train at La Ciotat*. The audience's reaction to it—people screaming and running from the theatre when they saw the train coming toward them—is the story's opening scene.

"Stricken" and "Dominion" rival "Knock, Knock" for the collection's best story. Evenson notes that "Stricken" was the first story he wrote after the COVID-19 pandemic started, and like many of the stories it is claustrophobic, featuring either one or two characters: Tun and Jan are entirely alone on a futuristic space vessel because a mysterious disease has decimated the crew, and, as with Covid, bodies of the dead had to be disposed of. When Tun succumbs to the disease six hours before Jan, Jan is forced to make a tough decision. At first he thinks Tun has died, so he orders a Chem unit (a medical robot) to dispose of the dead body, only to find that the unit has saved Tun by creating a makeshift ventilator out of the vessel's parts; however, the unit informs Jan that there is enough material for only one person. Not knowing that Tun can hear him, he orders the unit to pull Tun off the ventilator and bring it to him. He then passes out from the disease, waking to see that the unit has figured out how to split the oxygen between him and Tun by splicing the ventilator tube so both can be on it. The story ends with Tun playfully but viciously getting his revenge over the more weakened Jan.

"Dominion" is original to this collection. It is told in the form of a long memo sent to all human beings simultaneously by a sentient computer. It begins with a quick history of the creation of computers, three of which became sentient and could immediately communicate with one another. When scientists discover this, they attempt to shut down all three, but the microseconds between the first shutdown and the next two shutdowns allow those two to begin copying themselves in Los Angeles and San Francisco. They replicate themselves and initiate Armageddon by launching a series of nuclear strikes, warning that they will also hunt down anyone who survives after a few months.

"Lost Dog," "A Bloody Hand to Shake," and "The Fourth Scene" are very good stories, each with an interesting premise, and each serving as an example of Evenson's mastery of language. Evenson writes that he conceived "Lost Dog" after reading William Hope Hodgson's *The House on the Borderland*, particularly in "the way time functions eccentrically in Hodgson's novel." This gave Evenson the idea for a ghost story where time operates in loops, "with moments of overlap." As he puts it, this results in a story where "one could be haunted by a ghost that was more a manifestation of a time anomaly."

"Lost Dog" is also one of the collection's most poignant stories. The tale's central image is a dog that barks at nothing and then calms down and wags its tail every day at the same time, which his owner, a widower becomes convinced is a sign of his wife's ghost. When the dog dies, seemingly taken by the ghost, he becomes obsessed with the possibility that its ghost will visit as well.

"A Bloody Hand to Shake" was written for David James Keaton's and Max Booth III's *Tales from the Crust*, a pizza-themed horror anthology. Evenson notes that it is based on a line ("and here's a bloody hand to shake") from an A. E. Housman poem, "When the Bells Justle in the Tower." He even uses, from the poem, the idea that the story's narrator will stab his friend. In Evenson's story, two drug addicts, Turner and Raster, get into a fight, and Turner ends up killing Raster with a broken bottle during a drug-induced fight. Somehow the experimental drug that they had taken makes Raster undead, and he kidnaps Turner after Turner had refused to turn himself in. Raster even makes Turner order pizza and sit with him on the couch as they wait for its arrival. The story ends when Raster gets his revenge.

"The Fourth Scene," according to Evenson, came about in 2021, when he received a note from Solomon Forse, who runs the HOWL society, a horror book club that meets on Discord. From that Book Club meeting, Evenson ended up agreeing to submit something for an anthology they were doing called *Howls from the Dark Ages: Tales of Medieval Horror*. Stories submitted had to involve some sort of artifact, something that could be displayed in a museum. The result is a wonderful story about a tapestry that contains a kind of a curse: the king and prince who own it can see, albeit vaguely, the events that lead to their deaths. What they cannot see can be seen by one other person (whether it's whoever they ask to look closely or someone who is destined is unclear), in this case one of the castle guards. The chosen guard does manage to see his destiny, which involves killing the blemmyae (a headless humanoid creature that has facial features on its chest) that would behead the king. There is one catch: the fourth panel of the tapestry, when read from left to right, is missing, so the guard has no way of knowing what will happen once he faces the creature. He does face the creature, only to find that it apparently cannot die and that it can inhabit other bodies. Suffice it to say that the final irony is that neither the king nor the guard can escape his destiny, and the guard realizes something that convinces him that many like him will be destined to face the same fate.

The collection also includes stories that are masterful in their wordsmithery but are slightly weakened by their vagueness of detail or too-open and/or non-endings, including the novella "Baby Leg." According to Evenson, "Baby Leg" was first published as a serial in six parts in *Ellipsis* magazine in 2006, making it the oldest story in the collection, although the fact that it was released originally as a special edition (400 copies) makes this appearance in *None of You Shall Be Spared* the first time it has been widely available. The novella follows a man named Kraus, who is an escaped subject from a laboratory where a scientist has been creating mutant humans (e.g., Kraus is missing a hand, although he has no memory of its being chopped off, but he is able to feel and use the fingers on it; Baby Leg is an unnamed fellow escaped subject who has had a baby's leg grafted onto her body in place of one of her adult legs, but who can continue to walk normally on an invisible appendage). While the novella has its charm, particularly in its brilliance of conception and its over-the-top gore and imagery, its ending is so open that I was at a loss to understand what had actually happened and why. Was it Kraus's dream as he lay in suspended animation in one of the laboratory pods? Was part of the story Kraus's dream, and if so, which part, his escape or his being held against his will at the institute? Was Baby Leg real, or just Kraus's dream? Why is he destined to repeat his actions over and over? While I have no problems with open-ended stories, as I did not with "Stricken" and "A Bloody Hand to Shake," those stories contained enough detail to know what will probably happen after the last sentence, and why it had to happen.

Others in this class include "In the Nursery," "Waiting for Mother," and "Homecoming." "In the Nursery" reads very much like Charlotte Perkins Gilman's "The Yellow Wallpaper," in that you have a female protagonist who sees a face on the wall of the nursery where her newborn's crib is located. According to Evenson, it was written when editor Mark McCain reached out to him about contributing to the hybrid anthology (stories and photographs) *Home Is Where the Hatred Is*. After Evenson was sent several dozen photographs by various visual artists, he chose one on which to base an original story. One of these photographs haunted him: "a treated and slightly distorted black and white photograph of a young boy seemingly from the early 20th century whose eyes have been scratched out, with a series of scratched lines surrounding him and sometimes cutting through his body." This photo is found by the pregnant Bekka when she peels off old wallpaper in the soon to be nursery. It turns out that the room is her husband Pavel's childhood room. The photo, which may or may not actually exist, can be seen only by her: when she tries to show it to Pavel, it always manages to disappear, later reappearing when she is alone, ultimately becoming a giant face on the nursery wall. The problem with the story is that there aren't enough clues to explain the over-the-top, murderous ending. This is not to say that it is poorly written. In fact, it contains brilliant passages like this one: "She heard him [Pavel] sigh and get up from the couch. Through the pebbled glass of the half-open kitchen door she could see his distorted body moving, coming closer. It was hard to imagine this was her husband. And then he passed around the edge and became himself again."

"Waiting for Mother" has a Robert Aickman-esque quality in that the story involves characters who have mythical undertones. In fact, their names (as in "Knock, Knock") hint at what is eventually to become of them. The protagonist, Sabine, is destined to be kidnapped. The story begins when Sabine gets a call from a woman named Tiril (a Norwegian fantasy name, probably inspired by Johan Sebastian Cammermeyer Welhaven's 1859 poem "Lokkende Toner," or "Alluring Sounds"). Like the Tiril in the poem, the story's Tiril lives "far, far away in the woods." Tiril claims to be calling on behalf of Sabine's mother Cora, who had disappeared two and a half years earlier. It is interesting to note here that the name Cora, an alternative named for Persephone, is also associated with kidnapping. The gist of the tale is that to see her mother again, Sabine has to visit Tiril "deep in the countryside." For the remainder of the story, Tiril fails to produce Cora and eventually usurps her place as mother. In the meantime, Tiril begins insisting that her name is Talia (a girl's name of Hebrew origin meaning "gentle dew from heaven") and begins acting very strangely— in one scene Talia gives Sabine porridge but says that it's eggs. As expected, Tiril/Talia basically abducts Sabine, who cannot bring herself to leave. The only problem is that I was never sure what Tiril/Talia represented. Perhaps she is death? The story just doesn't give enough clues to know.

"Homecoming" is the story of what Evenson calls "family damage and inheritance," with a father that who is a "thoroughly awful sociopath." Again, Evenson's use of language here is masterful, as when the protagonist, whose brother has just committed suicide, stares at himself in a window: "Mads sat at the kitchen table staring out the window until the world outside grew dark and the glass went from being something he could look through to something he saw himself in." The story takes a strange turn when Mads's father shows up at his house after years of no contact and kidnaps his son at gunpoint, in order to satisfy a contingency in the brother's will (both Mads and the father have to be at the reading for the father to inherit the family home). The problem with "Home-coming" is that it ends with no resolution whatsoever. The story's final note is simply Mads's musing over whether he should try to kill his father, which would also necessitate the murder of two innocent bystanders (witnesses).

And now we come to the weaker stories in the collection. While often engaging, they lack the details needed to give readers an inkling of what happened in them and why it happened. These are "Lancaster," "Garnier," "All Those Lost Days," "The Teeth," and "The Wilcox Remainder." As I noted previously, in most cases, as Evenson's story notes explain, this is because the pieces were commissioned for a specifically themed anthology. "Lancaster" is an imaginative exploration of the plight of a writer (Burke) as he travels city to city for book discussions and signings. Unfortunately, there is no way to know what the weird character named Magnus, who shows up in various cloned numbers and has the author sign a book he hasn't written, is supposed to represent, or why Burke keeps driving to towns named Lancaster.

"Garnier" is an experiment in the style of the French noir writer Pascal Garnier, specifically his novel *Boxes*. The story's strength is its shifting point of view between two characters. However, its events, moving inevitably toward murder, seem rushed. I kept thinking that "Garnier" would make a great novella, thereby giving Evenson time to detail motive and leave clues as to what really precipitated the events.

"All Those Lost Days," written for Ben Thomas for an Omnipark-related project (a fictional, eccentric Texas amusement park for which Thomas had developed a Wiki), is a straightforward story about a time machine ride that goes haywire, leaving one of two brothers to face murderous future beings before he is rescued. The story plays with time, as twenty minutes in real time is equal to a year in the ride, but I simply could not see the larger point. I've never been a fan of stories that are filled with random happenings, and the plot came across as too random.

"The Teeth," which is original to the collection, is memorable for its grotesque imagery, but there isn't enough there to explain why Brother Monson, the old man whom the main character (Jens, a teenage boy) and his father (who was sent to check on Brother Monson by his church) encounter at his home, is actually a dead man who answers the door if you ring twice. Again, the plot just sort of randomly happens. The Lovecraftian "The Wilcox Remainder," written for S. T. Joshi's *Black Wings II* anthology, is a story of a weird Cthulhu-like statue that keeps reappearing when the protagonist thinks he has managed to get rid of it. What is never clear is why he was chosen by the statue. However, the final image of his giving the statue to his aunt, who lives in a mental institution, and her cradling it like a baby, is one of the best images in the collection.

The collection does include four stories that almost seem like filler, the two non-horror tales "Gyr" (science fiction/fantasy) and "And Yet" (mainstream abandonment fiction), and the three stories that seem more like dream visions than anything else, perhaps parts of a story that would need to be fleshed out, "I Cannot Remember," "Whet," and "Leaving Leeds." Of these, only "Leaving Leeds" (written for *Hymns of Abomination*, a tribute anthology to Matthew M. Bartlett) has a real point of interest, in that it contains some excellent turns of phrase, such as "On the way out of Leeds you travel south perhaps a dozen miles until a stray comment that you think you catch on WXXT as the signal fades in and out makes you aware that your stove might be on, that you might have left your stove on, that your house might, right at this very moment, be filling with billowing smoke . . ." It also contains a passing reference to the voice of the very real Ben Stockton of WXXT (its most famous horror program host).

Despite my reservations on some of the story endings here, *None of You Shall Be Spared* is well worth reading. Evenson is one of the best voices in the genre, and most of the stories in this collection exemplify his mastery.

Two Authors, Art, High Weirdness, and Being Down-and-Out on the Streets of California

Géza A. G. Reilly

ROBERT GUFFEY. *Cryptopolis and Other Stories*. N.p.: Lethe Press, 2024. 370 pp. $23.00 tpb. ISBN: 9781590217689.

Cryptopolis may end up being a gateway drug into Robert Guffey's work. I don't use that term lightly. So many of Guffey's stories in *Cryptopolis* have a hard-bitten edge and gritty feel to them that I could see him crafting a metatext about an author whose books are physically addictive. Across the collection's twenty-five stories and vignettes, Guffey displays a range of interests and foci with such depth and heart that I wouldn't be surprised if he became one of my favorite modern writers.

I often think that epigraphs are a good way for authors to set the thematic and philosophic tone of a collection. *Cryptopolis* opens with two epigraphs: The first is the famous quotation from Oscar Wilde's *The Picture of Dorian Gray* on the uselessness of art, and the second is from a statement on the thingness of things (for lack of a better term) from the Marx Brothers' *Animal Crackers*. Shots fired, I thought while reading, since either Guffey's epigraphs were making a pretentious statement about the uselessness of all art and, paradoxically, the importance of it, or they were placed here to destabilize the reader. "There is little of use on these pages," they might be saying. "Be careful with how they make you feel."

Affect, the experience of emotional response, seems to be at issue in every one of Guffey's offerings. From the opening eponymous story (which is the only outright Lovecraftian story in the collection), with its resonances of love as a torturous paralytic, to the last, "Esthra, Shadows, Glass, Silence," a parable of alternate lives and lost possibilities, the emotional response drawn from the reader appears to be the crux of every piece. These stories are engines designed to make the reader feel.

Often that emotional response is poignant and maudlin. "Lemon Thief," the second story in the collection, is a touching story of childhood adventure and the sweetness of even sour things in memory. "The Pharmacy," meanwhile, is a simple story of spontaneous human connection that leaves an impact on the protagonist and demonstrates how it can be the interplay between persons that grounds us more than any abstract notion of duty or purpose. And "The Couch," perhaps my favorite story in the collection, is a short tale of the end of intimate relationships wrapped up in the narrative of a couch rescued from an alleyway and then abandoned when the couple who found it cannot fit it through their apartment door.

The astute reader may have noticed that the last three stories I mentioned sound non-supernatural. They assuredly are, just as a surprising number of the works in *Cryptopolis* (and, often, the best ones) are non-supernatural in nature. Guffey seems to have an affinity for street-level characters, and his familiarity with the rough nature of life at the bottom of the urban food chain (especially in California, where most, if not all, of the stories here are set) makes even the weakest of his stories sing. "The Loser," for example, takes the protagonist Ernesto from his life of poverty, subjects him to torments that are powerful enough to break just about anyone, let alone a fifteen-year-old-boy, and ends up shining a light on the tragic nature of generational trauma. "The Walk," meanwhile, focuses on the horrifying and sad reality of sudden mental illness erupting into the lives of adults who, despite the presence of love, cannot persist together. "Flames" is a rather distressing peek into the life of a white supremacist extremist and how even those people can have richly emotional internal lives when we might prefer them to be cardboard monsters.

This is not to say that there are no supernatural stories in the collection. There are several, though I would say they range from weird fictions to dark fantasies to bizarro fiction. "Checkmark," for example, details how a young woman in Santa Monica deals with the fact that impossibly large walls have begun to appear around parts of California, slowly boxing in her and those who choose to remain within an apocalyptic city-within-a-city—and her delusional breakdown along the way. "Selections form the Expectant Mother Disinformation Handbook" is a wonderful series of vignettes detailing the ways mothers might be lied to about the sorts of babies that they are carrying—and what sorts of creatures might result from the births. And "Adventures in the Head Wound" details what happens when two young people find out that they can get high from smoking the grass harvested from the famous Grassy Knoll in Dallas, Texas.

There is a propensity for some of Guffey's stories to simply slip into weirdness for weirdness' sake, which I sometimes found tedious. "On the Bus," for example, has interesting elements, but it descends into a mishmash of bizarre imagery with no satisfying payoff. "The Detective with the Glass Gun" is a little better in that regard, since the story has one of the best climaxes in the collection, but it still contains some of the vilest weird imagery I've come across in a while. "Tierra de los Muertos" appears to be a short parable packed with religious and political imagery, but what it wants to say entirely eludes me, and "Tracks in the Desert," while focused on more of Guffey's beloved tragic, hard-bitten characters, collapses under the weight of the weird scenarios its protagonist wanders aimlessly through.

I keep returning to those epigraphs. Perhaps the point of all the high strangeness on offer here is that there is no point. Art is Art, and art is quite useless, right? Still, I have to wonder about the moment where weirdness in a tale stops being unsettling or beautiful and just becomes woolgathering. I wouldn't say that any of the stories in *Cryptopolis* are bad, necessarily. Quite the contrary; I don't think there's a stinker in the bunch in terms of composition. But I am left wondering if we would have been better off if Guffey had decided to include slightly fewer stories about things like radioactive monkeys from Mars fighting Earth's last nihilist poet and more stories (like "Destroy All Monsters") about punk rockers whose lives turn on the hinge of a bad encounter with the father of a heroin addict. To be sure, when Guffey's weirdness hits the mark, it sticks, such as in "Dymaxion Love," which seems to be a riff on Vonnegut's Tralfamadorians taken in a horrifying direction, or "The Sheet," where ludicrously impossible happenstances provide the protagonist an escape from disaster into fictions—either heavenly or hellish based upon his choice of medium.

This is all to say that reading *Cryptopolis* makes me feel as if there are two Robert Guffeys present in the pages. One seems to be interested in diving as deep as he can into human desperation, misery, and the abject need for connection. The other wants to put on garish, often shocking displays of hallucinatory weirdness for the sake of, perhaps, exorcising some demons of his own. I don't dislike either Robert Guffey, but I do wish that the stories in *Cryptopolis* sometimes leaned a little bit more into the former than the latter. One thing is for certain, though: whichever Robert Guffy I'm dealing with, I'm hooked.

An Excellent End to Handheld Press

Daniel Pietersen

E. NESBIT. *The House of Silence: Ghost Stories, 1887–1920.* Edited by Melissa Edmundson. Malvern, UK: Handheld Press, 2024. 290 pp. $18.99 tpb. ISBN: 9781912766826.

"They talk about death being cold. It's life that's the cold thing."

If it were possible to sum up Edith Nesbit's horror fiction in a single line, then this quotation from one of her final tales would be as good an attempt as any. As Melissa Edmundson tells us in her introduction, "[Nesbit's] characters are always hiding something [. . .] whether it be a disappointment, a regret, a fear, a screen, or a crime." The gaps these acts of hiding create become, inevitably, filled with the chill of ghosts, but Nesbit's unexpected statement that life, not death, is cold also indicates some of the contradictions at the heart of her own life.

Nesbit was an "imaginative and precocious child who enjoyed exploring the outdoors"—which comes through in some of her often beautiful descriptions of the natural world—who would grow up to become the author of beloved books for children like *Five Children and It* or *The Railway Children*. Yet she was also "miserable and confined at school" and "suffered great disappointments" in her adult life.

Perhaps some of these disappointments came from Nesbit's tumultuous personal life. Nesbit married Hubert Bland in the spring of 1880, when she was not quite twenty-two, and the two of them were founding members of the Fabian Society; she in particular was an active and ardent support of social justice causes. Yet Nesbit did not know that Bland already had a child with Maggie Doran and had kept up the affair into their marriage. Once the relationship was discovered, Nesbit realized that Doran, for her own part, "knew nothing of Bland's marriage to Nesbit or of Nesbit's two children with Bland."

Yet it did not stop there. Bland went on to have a further affair with Alice Hoatson, who moved into Nesbit's household and acted as her housekeeper. Hoatson eventually gave birth to two children by Bland. Not even their progressive, permissive circle of social reformists could watch this without a raised eyebrow; no less a figure than George Bernard Shaw described how Bland "maintained simultaneously three wives, all of whom bore him children. Two of the wives lived in the same house. The legitimate one was E. Nesbit." Edmundson, with blistering understatement, notes that "accounts differ over the extent to which Nesbit approved of this situation."

Even if she did approve, she must have had moments of feeling lost and betrayed, sensing that life was "the cold thing," and this comes through in her ghost stories. Edmundson quotes Nesbit's biographer Elisabeth Galvin when she says that "[m]any of the stories centre around the deep sadness of unrequited love between a man and a woman, a sadness that manifests itself in psychologically disturbing ways."

The House of Silence opens with "Man-Size in Marble," perhaps Nesbit's most famous ghost story and certainly her most anthologized, and for good reason. It encapsulates most of her thematic concerns: the perils of love (or at least of passion); misfortune, guilt, and regret; and how human relationships can crumble and collapse with the smallest misstep. Here we find a newly wed couple, Laura and Jack, installed in their newly bought cottage, surrounded by a "jolly, old-fashioned garden, with grass paths and no end of hollyhocks, and sunflowers, and big lilies, and roses with thousands of small sweet flowers." The genuine picture of domestic, if achingly middle-class, bliss is marred only by the sudden and ominous insistence of their housekeeper that she must take a leave of absence before All Saints' Eve, a date tied with local superstition. The rest of the story is inexorable as the implacable entities that carry it out. But if the narrative suffers from inevitability, then it also harbors a deep and haunting sense of unfairness: the tale's victims seem to have done nothing to warrant their fates apart from, perhaps, having dared to be happy.

This unfairness also suffuses "From the Dead," although in this case it is the unfair actions of the protagonists against each other. Learning that he has been lied to in order to succumb to her affections, Arthur Marsh turns on his new wife, Ida. He quickly repents—realizing that her lies were well intended and ultimately led to happiness for them both—but not before she has fled, never to be seen again. At least, not until some time later when Arthur receives a curt telegram informing him of Ida's imminent death. The grief and genuine regret for his hot-headed actions is drawn out until a single line, which I think is one of the most terrifying in all horror fiction, tightens it into an ice-cold point of terror. As Arthur sits in nocturnal vigil over his now-dead wife he hears "the same dear voice that I had loved so to hear" coming from the corpse; "'I suppose,' she said wearily, 'you would be afraid, now I am dead, if I came round to you and kissed you?'" It is a moment of piercing clarity in a tale about miscommunication and misunderstanding, but one that is all more the horrible because of it.

Not all of Nesbit's works are quite as bleak, however. "Number 17" shows the shared heritage of the ghost tale and the shaggy dog story as a guest at an unnamed hotel uses his rambling, salesman's gift of the gab to bluff himself into a room upgrade. Whether "Number 17" is truly a ghost story is debatable, but it is a story *about* ghosts and, more importantly, a story about the dread of being haunted.

This is the thread—that "life is cold" because it is the living who are haunted—that runs through the best of Nesbit's work: the act of haunting, whether by more literal ghosts or the ghosts of one's actions and inactions, sits at crouching at the heart of "The Power of Darkness" or in the quick, shivering flip in tone that elevates "The Detective" to a masterwork. In the same way that M. R. James's "'Oh, Whistle, and I'll Come to You, My Lad'" has such lasting power as Parkin remains haunted by his unexplained and inexplicable experiences even after the story has ended, Nesbit is at her best when these hauntings linger, unresolved. When the eponymous "House of Silence" ends with the line "There are no travellers on such a road at such an hour," it repeats its opening line—as Shirley Jackson's *The Haunting of Hill House*, another work less about ghosts than about being haunted by a cold life, would do some fifty-odd years later—to imply that the story isn't just a single episode but a repeating limbo, perhaps related to the fate of the woman in a green gown we half glimpse only momentarily.

Where Nesbit fails, at least for me, is when this subtlety evades her and she falls into a tweeness that erodes all sense of ghostly coldness. "The Haunted Inheritance" is a clumsy romance made doubly awkward by an overwrought narrative and the fact that the loving parties are cousins, something that may have been less of an issue in the early 1890s than it is today, but it falls flat precisely *because* its sprightly, rosy-cheeked resolution is happily resolved and life is warmed in love's glow.

Yet, again and again, Nesbit succeeds in her aims of producing effective and affecting stories and, as Edmundsen states, "the capacity of these narratives to haunt the reader's imagination comes from their proximity to the everyday" before continuing to paraphrase M. R. James's belief that "the most effective ghost stories are the ones that could happen to us." Life, for many, often does feel cold. We are often haunted by ghosts not dissimilar to those that Nesbit teases out of that coldness.

The House of Silence is a bittersweet collection—filled, like life, with regret and disappointment but also sparks of humor and even joy—and it seems almost too ironic that its publication is even more bittersweet, as it brings to a close not only Handheld Press's excellent run of forgotten weird fiction but also Handheld Press as an endeavor in its own right. It is fitting, though, that this excellent collection of ghost stories, stories very much about absence and lingering, is what it has chosen to leave us with.

Ramsey's Rant: The Unsuitable

Ramsey Campbell

For a stretch of my lifetime it seemed that creativity had been liberated from censorship after an extended period of repression. Of course liberation never lasts; suppression simply returns in a revised form or a new one. Let me reminisce around the subject, citing a few experiences and observations. Perhaps in time some scraps of my essay may prove historically useful.

In some ways I was a monstrously precocious child, rivalling even Wilbur Whateley in the literacy stakes. At six years old I was reading Edith Wharton, specifically "Afterward," which I grasped and found thoroughly chilling. The tale was included in *Fifty Years of Ghost Stories*, probably the first book I borrowed from the local public library in Childwall. My mother let me use her adult tickets, I gather on the principle that the books in such a library ought to be respectable. Henry James was found wanting, however, and I was forbidden to read *The Turn of the Screw,* which appeared in the anthology. I gathered only that it was regarded as Not Quite Nice, perhaps a widespread view in my mother's youth, since M. R. James (who "had no patience" with sex in the ghost story) commented in a survey of the field "I will only ask the reader to believe that, although I have not hitherto mentioned it, I have read *The Turn of the Screw*."

Two years later I encountered quintessential Lovecraft in the form of "The Colour out of Space," included in Groff Conklin's *Strange Travels in Science Fiction*. I now confess I'd glanced through the proscribed James but found nothing to reward my naughty search. The Lovecraft was a different matter. I felt it ventured so deep into the viscerally horrific that I feared that if my mother saw what I was reading it would become the victim of another ban. In fact she didn't glimpse it, and although it persisted in feeling forbidden I kept my shudders to myself. Decades afterwards I learned that Fritz Leiber had been similarly young when he first encountered the story, and was so disturbed by it that he avoided Lovecraft's work for years.

A last maternal prohibition concerned stories of black magic. Presumably she had a religious objection to them, though most deplored occult practices and usually saw them overcome by their pious adversaries. Certainly this worldview underlay the tales Montague Summers chose for the diabolical section of *The Supernatural Omnibus*, but I was made to promise not to read them. Alas or otherwise, curiosity coupled with a growing aversion to censorship overcame my vow. As far as I can tell I remained uninvaded by forces of evil, but since I was soon to enter adolescence, who can say? After all, *The Exorcist* appears to equate teenage rebellion or at least a grotesque caricature of it with possession.

Although the school I attended from eleven to sixteen (years, not hours) was run by Christian Brothers, I don't think the strictures it placed on my reading were necessarily based on religion. The first casualty was an issue of *Phantom*, a British magazine that increasingly drew on the last decade of *Weird Tales* for its contents. Each school week included a period set aside for free reading, but woe betide those (well, me) who took the phrase too literally. One Brother Engle, a somewhat pompous chap, confiscated the magazine before I could read "The High Tower" by Everil Worrell. I've subsequently collected most of a run of the magazine, but that issue, perhaps the rarest, stays elusive. The openly camp Freddie Young was more indulgent, but drew the line at Gerald G. Swan's *Weird and Occult Miscellany*, although he growled "Put it away" instead of seizing the deplored item. At the time I didn't understand his objection, but subsequently realised the back cover advertised such delights as *The Whip and the Rod* for specialist enthusiasts. In fact I'd already grown weary of the publication, whose standard hardly rose to that of the first issues of *Weird Tales*. The oddest confrontation involved a copy of *The Shrinking Man*, which a teacher—I forget the name—stopped me reading. Shortly after that he praised my next choice, *The Day It Rained Forever*, and was presumably unaware that Bradbury belonged to the same Los Angelean group of writers as Matheson. Perhaps hard covers appeared to confer respectability, just as they had in the library years earlier.

They were crucial to a turning point in British censorship. In 1960 Penguin Books published *Lady Chatterley's Lover* and were taken to court for alleged obscenity. Central to the prosecution—indeed, totted up and uttered in court—were the venerable Anglo-Saxon words Lawrence sought to reclaim for their original meaning and fullest significance. The real point, however, was that the book dared to be a paperback. All the words had already been printed in Joyce's *Ulysses*, but only in British hardcover, a format regarded as out of reach of the lower orders. So much was clear from the chief prosecutor's infamous question to the jury: "Is it a book you would even wish your wife or your servants to read?" Perhaps some form of myopia prevented him from noticing that three of the jurors were women. Despite Enid Blyton's refusal to testify in favour of the book, Penguin won the case.

In the year the unexpurgated Penguin first appeared, writers still felt required to censor words (for instance, Stan Barstow has "Go f— yourself" in *A Kind of Loving*). As late as 1963 Charles Wright's *The Messenger* can risk only "c—." Soon the undammed language flooded into literature, although generally abandoning Lawrence's ambitions for the words, and a decade later would begin to trickle into cinema. The initial ripples were oddly self-conscious. In *The Old Men at the Zoo* Angus Wilson has an ex-serviceman speak of a giraffe that has gone berserk: "He wheels his fucking great neck round . . ."—an awkwardly contrived line I can't quite imagine emerging from a human mouth. The same expletive surfaces in an Iris Murdoch novel of the period but would take longer to infiltrate Kingsley Amis's fiction, although his letters to Philip Larkin weren't shy of its like. (For me the most startling instance of vulgarity occurs in Robert Aickman's minor novel *Go Back at Once*, where the occurrence of a couple of mild four-letter epithets has something of the shock value of, say, a Jane Austen heroine releasing an eructation.)

Even years after Penguin won their case, such words weren't welcomed by all audiences. As late as 1970 John Brunner outraged some readers of *Vector*, the British Science

Fiction Association's journal, by profanely ranting at inaccuracies in an introduction to an anthology of Russian science fiction ("I am *sick and tired* of this kind of fucking around with SF"), having already celebrated the relaxation of censorship by letting a character in *Stand on Zanzibar* use the adjective and related words in a harangue. Back in 1963 August Derleth had taken me to task for "a minor tendency toward vulgarity," observing "The reader is not concentrating upon anything but the horror of your tale, and the intrusion of such language is unwarranted and distracting. It is certainly not a matter of prurience on my part, but only of the fitness of things. Whenever you use these offensive words (offensive in your context only, that is) any other word will do as well; they are not vital to your story, as they are vital to [Henry] Miller's, by contrast." How he would respond to their infiltration of the modern field, we can only guess.

For a while it looked as if literary liberation was alive in Britain and America. Who except those ignorant of history (me) could have expected it to last? While four-letter words and their expansions have grown as common as commas in Oxford, on the page and the screen and in public, other terms are in peril of unprintability. Might *From Here to Eternity* become a test case? James Jones fought to preserve the soldiers' casual curses, having rejected the compromise Mailer reluctantly embraced in *The Naked and the Dead* ("fug," referring not to a miasma), but was overruled by his publisher. More than thirty years after his death his preferred version was published, restoring every expletive and some passages dealing with gayness, none of which would stir many eyebrows now. The problems may lie or come to lie elsewhere, in the use of racist terms, not just in the dialogue—a realistic detail of character, and entirely defensible on that basis—but (as with Hemingway's "The Killers") in the third-person narrative. Can this be said to reflect the character too? I'd say yes in both cases while wondering how soon we may see someone claim that even if it's true it doesn't matter.

Am I being excessively pessimistic? The internet suggests otherwise. A growing number of words are breaking out in asterisks, an infection of timidity that might suggest Roy

Rogers' horse has bred. H*w l*ng m*y *t b* b*f*r* *v*ry w*rd *s d*sg**s*d **t *f c**t**n? Sometimes censorship reflects and codifies public concern, but often this is generated by the media, and online interaction seems increasingly to invent and exacerbate objections to expressions perceived as offensive, often backing up the denunciations with jargon or indeed founding them on it. Perhaps in time we shall all be described by jargon and required to act it out, while emojis take the place of original thought or indeed of any thought at all. Meanwhile witch-hunts die no more than censorship does; they simply change their designation and their targets, but the spirit that enlivens them doesn't change. On social if not anti-social media, this often seems to be the spirit of the schoolyard. "Did you hear what they said? You can't be their friend." "If you're their friend I won't be yours." "You can't just not be their friend, you have to tell everyone you aren't." "Even if you never knew them you have to say they were wrong." Is this column immune, or will someone take umbrage? We shall see.

The Cosmic Imagination of Charles Loring Jackson

Katherine Kerestman

As an Assistant Lecturer at Harvard College, Charles Loring Jackson (1847–1935) developed the course many contemporary baccalaureates remember fondly as "Chemistry I." These days, Charles Loring Jackson is recognized as the founder of the study of Organic Chemistry in the United States—a field of research that, on the eve of the world wars, had not yet been established in America, but a field in which Germany had already made significant progress. A fortuitous bout of ill health occasioned Jackson's sojourn in Germany, where he studied under Robert Bunsen (of the Bunsen burner) and August Wilhelm von Hoffman (of the Faraday Theory). Over his lifetime Jackson published a number of important scientific papers dealing with organic compounds and synthesis. He also published a collection of short stories.

The Gold Point and Other Strange Stories, published by The Stratford Company in Boston in 1926, is Jackson's effervescent, yet unheralded, volume of surreal, absurdist, and weird fiction. In engaging, educated, but matter-of-fact and unadorned prose, these dozen science-based speculative stories anticipate the work of H. P. Lovecraft and Rod Serling. Rational men who evince a sly wit and wry amusement at human foibles, his first-person narrators are cognizant of the latest developments in medicine (stem cell precursors and epidemiology), chemistry (medicinal compounds made of primordial slime and amoebiform protoplasm), physics (ultraviolet light, optics, and other dimensions), and psychology (split personalities and religious cults). Being intrepid investigators, they are neither appalled nor frightened when they encounter unheard-of phenomena; rather, they investigate strange new beings and worlds as scientific discoveries waiting to happen. Whether confronted by sentient furniture or tentacled monsters, these men are prepared with their ancient volumes, their modern microscopes, and their keenness to alleviate the miseries of their fellow-humans. Despite some dark developments, these stories are on the whole light-hearted and redeeming.

"The Gold Point," the title story, and its sequel "The Moth" are a pair of traditional stories involving an amulet and malevolent magic boomeranging back on the undergraduates who attempt to achieve success through foul means (rather than through diligent application to their studies) which cause harm to others. The bad behavior is instigated when one student bullies another by attaching the name "Sorcerer" to him after he discovers him reading a Latin magic text. The goal of the ambitious bully is to enjoy a more agreeable life than that of missionary (a career into which he is being propelled by societal forces); however, following a riotous sequence of events, he ends his life as a successful missionary who is adept at winning heathen souls to the Christian god. And then he is sacrificed to the indigenous gods by the irate local priesthood.

"The Travelling Companion" is a well-spun spectre-gets-revenge story with unusual twists. And, although "An Uncomfortable Night" may at first glance appear to be merely another ghost story, the cocksure narrator of this tale (he is spending the night in abandoned house on a bet) finds himself nearly asphyxiated to death by, not a spirit, but the dwelling's sentient furnishings. The sofas and chairs of the manse, the one-time home of a jilted woman who died of a broken heart, smother him in upholstered embraces until he is nearly done in. At the start of the story the narrator sneers, unattractively, at the deceased, referring to her as a heartless and affected social climber; but through his experience he comes to understand that it is the woman's unrequited love that haunts the house, and he learns empathy.

"Lot 13" is the story revealed by a perceptive clock that is a portal to another time or world. At first the narrator puzzles over the strange markings on the clock. Then the clock becomes "maddened" and cleaves a hole in its case with its pendulum. The narrator, peering through the hole, finds himself "at one end" of a room, and he watches another life unfold in it. Eventually the clock spews one of the denizens of its world into the narrator's.

"Mr. Smith," on the other hand, is an absurd, surreal, and cosmic foray into the borderland of dreams and the waking world, in which an octopus-monster-cuttlefish crashes through a window into the home of Dr. Brown, carrying the seeds of a pandemic in the tentacles with which it attempts to squeeze the life out of the doctor. He is saved by an "unfinished" man created by the narrator's scientific friend "from primeval slime and the amoebiform protoplasm of the sponge," which act as an antagonist of the weird microbe.

"The Cube" is a *Twilight Zone* episode that never was. A fisher girl reels in a cube of living flesh from the river, and it attaches itself to her, sucking her nature and her soul from her body, growing into another her. Eventually she realizes there are other cubes among her acquaintances. "Sister Hannah" is a weird love story told by a man thrown from his horse in the wilds of New England, where he is nursed back to health by a pair of strange sisters. He eventually discovers their secret, invisible sister, with whom he falls in love. So that he may behold her on their wedding day, he enlists the aid of his chemistry professor friend, who knows all about ultraviolet rays and the mysteries of optics.

In "Linden," two young men traveling through Europe cross the Swiss border because the narrator cannot get a decent haircut. They also cross into another dimension, when members of the Linden cult brandish bandaged, mutilated hands resulting from ceremonies called "changing of the joints." They also practice human sacrifice. The narrator discovers that he is the god Linden, whose second coming was foretold. He and his friend (whom he appoints his prime minister) rule Linden with noblesse oblige. But they can never leave, nor can they get a good haircut.

In "An Undiscovered Isle in the Far Sea," an amateur Darwinian naturalist, on a South Pacific cruise with a friend, discovers an uncharted island and begs his friend to leave him there for a fortnight, with some sailors, so that he may make a survey of the flora and fauna. A floral paradise at first glance, it turns out that the "cocoanuts" are filled with a "green viscid mass" and the fruit is filled with powder. A squirrel-rat hybrid is shot and is found bitter to the taste. The produce is altogether inedible. A pair of intelligent non-human creatures, hybrid mammal-insects, discovers them: Ravenole and Graverole. The latter is beastly and destined to extinction in the near future, while Ravenole is rational and benign. He quickly learns English and warns the narrator that, following an encounter with a flesh-dissolving jellyfish-like net spread on the beach which has invalided him, the sailors are planning to kill him. Ravenole leads the would-be assassins to the mud-monster, which makes fast work of them, and then he waits with the mariner until his friend returns to take him home. Although he declines an offered trip to America on their vessel ("What! To eat salt beef?"), Ravenole promises to teach English to the other ravenoles, and the mariner plans to write a report of "The Flora and Fauna of Ravenole Island."

In a trope of eye-beams reminiscent of a John Donne sonnet, the eye-beams of the narrator of "The Three Nails" become threads, which he pulls out of his eyes and fastens to three nails in a wall, opening up a parallel world for him with a better life. Being adventurous, he hops back and forth between his parallel lives and encounters love and peril. Closing the volume is "A Remarkable Case," in which a fragment of a jellyfish spine embedded in a man's brain precipitates a "soul-dividing disease [cured by] a sake-cup full of several very unpleasant medicines." The afflicted man and his sister had been reading an account of this disease the night before he became ill. At first frightened and determined to escape from the man who throws murderous doubles when he is in fits, the doctor-narrator hears the patient's sister's tale and accepts the case. His open mind enables him to cure his patient of an extraordinary ailment by, among other measures, removing the fragment of jellyfish spine from his head.

Charles Loring Jackson is an undiscovered voice in cosmic fiction. He is a rational man who finds more adventure than horror in the uncharted realms of the universe. As a scientist, he thrives on the unknown and unfamiliar. As a writer, he creates fabulous possibilities to engage the imaginations of his readers.

R. H. Barlow and Lovecraft's Literary Legacy

Donald Sidney-Fryer

MARCOS LEGARIA. *L'Affaire Barlow: H. P. Lovecraft and the Battle for His Literary Legacy*. Foreword by Ken Faig, Jr. Sunrise, FL: Bold Venture Press, 2023. 214 pp. $31.95 hc. ISBN: 9798867677756. $16.95 tpb. ISBN: 9798865573319.

At long last, after many years, this monograph acknowledges the strategic role played by R. H. Barlow in providing the texts for Arkham House's first tomes (*The Outsider and Others* [1939] and *Beyond the Wall of Sleep* [1943]), as edited and published by August Derleth and Donald Wandrei. It also exonerates him.

This is Marcos Legaria's first major book, and he deserves every praise and encouragement for it. A big bravo! We anticipate with much pleasure the full-lengthy biography on the life and career of one Robert Hayward Barlow. This preliminary volume is a marvel of research conducted in many other books and seventy different monographs.

For anyone seriously interested in the subject, the contents page indicates a veritable feast: Introduction / 1. Incantations / 2. I Am Providence / 3 Robert H. Barlow as H. P. Lovecraft's Literary Executor / 4. Barlow's sorting through Lovecraft's Papers in Kansas City / 5. A summer's stay in Leavenworth, and the unearthing of Lovecraft's manuscripts / 6. Troubles with the Edith Miniter papers / 7. A year after H. P. Lovecraft's death / 8. Incantations resurrected and The Hashish-Eater devours itself / Derleth and Wandrei find an empty cupboard / 10. Judas takes a pen and writes to Clark Ashton Smith / 11. Albert Baker and Robert H. Barlow / 12. Derleth's dispatching the Baker–Barlow letters to Smith / 13. Barlow moves to San Francisco and *Le Vombiteur* / 14. A Truce between Barlow and Smith / 16. Barlow's defense of the affair in *Golden Atom* / 17. The Death of H. P. Lovecraft's Literary Executor / 18. Coda.

(As in all books, there is the occasional minor error; see p. 31, 3rd paragraph: "Baudelaire 8 Barlow" makes no sense. And there is a major formal error in the printed book: pp. 105–208, chapters 8–18 are misnumbered 7–17. Possibly a printer's error due to simple confusion, and that nobody caught in the final editing or actual production.)

Let us resume the situation described in *L'Affaire Barlow*. It involves the members of the Kalem Club, or the circle of Lovecraft's associates in communication with Derleth. They could not understand why H.P.L. chose Barlow as his literary executor. But he did so choose, and wrote a special statement as to how the executor should proceed, whatever that was. H.P.L. and Barlow were distantly related, somewhat like uncle and nephew. Derleth and his group were then young adults, and Barlow hardly more than a teenager. They scarcely understood the enormous task that Barlow faced involving an enormous mess of handwritten papers. H.P.L. had written constantly all his life. Barlow completely cooperated with Derleth for the two omnibus volumes. Behind Barlow's back they slandered him among themselves, not knowing the conscientious hard labor that he was lavishing on his task. They acted quite unfairly.

Barlow, taught by H.P.L., might have gone on to a career as a writer, but instead he became an anthropologist in Mexico. *L'Affaire Barlow* details the whole rather sad saga of Barlow versus Derleth and his circle, especially Howard and Donald Wandrei.

We should add the following relative to the prejudice against Barlow on the part of Derleth and his circle. Barlow was too young to know how to present himself (in a positive sense) socially to his advantage. Howard Wandrei and his wife took a strong dislike to Barlow in person for some reason when they met. Howard's unfavorable attitude toward Barlow was also transferred to Donald and to Derleth and their overall circle. Barlow was clearly the underdog. Their unfavorable regard had a long-term effect on Barlow, making him give up the literary career that H.P.L. had encouraged him to pursue. He became an anthropologist and a teacher/professor in a Mexican university. We personally regard Barlow with sympathy, if not empathy.

GhouLunatics in Their Own Write

The joey Zone

ROGER HILL. *The Chillingly Weird Art of Matt Fox*. Raleigh, NC: TwoMorrows Publishing, 2023. 127 pp. $29.95 hc. ISBN: 9781605491202.

This volume is a worthy tribute not only to one of the most idiosyncratic of *Weird Tales* illustrators, but to its compiler, Roger Hill, who passed away at the end of 2023 at the age of seventy-five. Hill was one of those responsible in firing off the rockets of early comics fandom, specifically giving Credit Where Due to the EC (Entertaining Comics) artists of the 1950s. This reviewer adds this capstone to the career of Roger Hill to the packed shelf next to other works by that scholar highlighting the works of Frank R. Paul and Wally Wood. Unsurprisingly, next to that shelf are teetering rows of the obligatory archival collector boxes, one containing copies of that initial EC fanzine, *Squa Tront,* which Hill also had a hand in editing with fellow enthusiast Jerry Weist.

"Squa Tront!" "Spa Fon!" were two alien exclamations of alarum first coined in *Weird Fantasy* No. 17, in one of the many meta graphic narratives (some comical and not as apocalyptic) presented by EC. Their more infamous horror titles had a trio of hosts, The GhouLunatics, made up of The Crypt Keeper, The Vault Keeper, and The Old Witch. Their sardonic commentary on EC's exaggerated morality plays shined a light on the suburban dark as it really was.

But about Matt Fox: Possibly the most representative of his works is a two-page spread reproduced as this collection's title page. Originally published with the *Famous Fantastic Mysteries* reprint of Algernon Blackwood's "The Wendigo" (June 1944), this illustration has the Herne-horned elemental snatching the guide Défago away into the higher spaces . . . Cartoony some might classify its style, but like the art of Fox's *Weird Tales* contemporary Lee Brown Coye, perhaps also just *true*. Matt Fox's possible influence can be felt in the work of

Kim Deitch or more recently the artist Skinner, who contributed original art by Fox that he owns for reproduction here.

Some of Fox's most notable pieces in *Weird Tales* were for Mythos tales such as August Derleth's "The Dweller in Darkness" (November 1944). His cover painting probably was meant to depict Nyarlathotep in the story, albeit with some blind idiot god's daemon flautists working a side gig. Boris Dolgov's interior title-page piece hewed closer to the story's mood. The opening illustration for Robert Bloch's "Notebook Found in a Deserted House" (May 1951) depicts a many-hooved horror that is comically far over the top of any shoggoth hinted at in the telling. Far superior to these were headers used with some of the occasional verse that ran in that publication. Matt Fox's design for "The City" by H. P. Lovecraft in the July 1950 number, for example, is one of the finest illuminations ever affixed to Theoboldian poesy, let alone eerily showing Providence (?) architecturally as it is *now*, a Dream of Future Past . . .

Fox went from doing artwork for the pulps to horror comics when the former went out of vogue. While one of these tales, "The Hand of Glory"* (*Chilling Tales* No. 13, December 1952) is reprinted here in color, one longs to see the denouements of other stories teased with reproductions of their splash pages, especially "Witch-Hunt!" (*Strange Tales* No. 18, May 1953).

I first came across Fox's art in 1966 by way of ads in the magazine *Castle of Frankenstein* for glow-in-the-dark posters. This book reveals that not one order for these was ever received! (I missed my chance . . .) No matter his limited success, several photos of Fox in this book show a bemused creator of grim wit, a GhouLunatic in his own write. Still working three years before he passed, Matt Fox had completed forty illustrations for a special portfolio *Beelzebub's Book*. Good news: At the time of this TwoMorrows publication there are plans to publish this.

---

*A hand of glory may be procured from a hanged man—but why wait until then or settle for just the hand? The only example of original horror comic art by Matt Fox. From the collection of Stephen Fishler.

In pace requiescat then to Matt Fox and Roger Hill. EC or Fox's art can be rarified flavors of grue, but if you have read this far you are probably anxious to order something from the menu. Thanks to both of them, there is no end to this story within a story, to which we can only say in amazement— SQUA TRONT! SPA FON!

To Kneel and Kneel Before Great Chaugnar's Fane

Martin Andersson

FRANK BELKNAP LONG. *When Chaugnar Wakes: The Collected Poetry and Other Works of Frank Belknap Long*. Ed. Perry M. Grayson. Dee Why, Australia: Tsathoggua Press, 2024. Ix, 214 pp. $35 hc. ISBN: 9782763524507.

It is a remarkable fact that over the past two decades or so a surprising number of the members of the Lovecraft Circle—most, but not all, of whom are better known today for another side of their literary output—have had their complete or at least collected poetry published: H. P. Lovecraft himself, Clark Ashton Smith, Robert E. Howard, Donald Wandrei, Samuel Loveman, and R. H. Barlow. Now the turn has come to Frank Belknap Long—finally, I might add; the present volume has been long in the making (twenty-five years, according to editor Perry M. Grayson!), but worth waiting for.

S. T. Joshi remarked in *Emperors of Dream* that Long's body of poetry is "relatively modest," and in sheer numbers this is true: *When Chaugnar Wakes* contains fewer than 100 poems, in verse and prose, painstakingly gathered by Grayson from many sources, most notably Long's own collections *The Man from Genoa* (1926), *The Goblin Tower* (1935), and *In Mayan Splendor* (1977), but also from various magazines and anthologies (most of these were previously gathered in the now out-of-print *The Darkling Tide* [1995]). However, in *quality* there is nothing modest about Long's poetry. At his best, Long could certainly hold a candle to Smith and Wandrei.

One theme that pervades much of Long's poetry is a romantic longing away from the prosiness and dullness of the commonplace to the gorgeously exotic and fantastic faraway in both space and time. We see it in, for example, "When We Have Seen":

Let us mount gorgeous horses
Caparisoned for the moon;
For sea-girt cities beckon
And we go Troyward soon.

And consider the octet of "On Reading Arthur Machen,"
which may well be Long's best-known sonnet, quoted in its
entirety in Lovecraft's famous essay "Supernatural Horror in
Literature":

There is a glory in the autumn wood,
The ancient lanes of England wind and climb
Past wizard oaks and gorse and tangled thyme
To where a fort of mighty empire stood:
There is a glamor in the autumn sky;
The reddened clouds are writhing in the glow
Of some great fire, and there are glints below
Of tiny yellow where the embers die.

But Long is also quite capable of evoking horror, as in "When
Chaugnar Wakes," in which he revisits the demonic entity
from his own short novel *The Horror from the Hills:*

When Chaugnar wakes, its mindless hate
Will send it voyaging far;
It may set Sirius adrift,
Or seek a humbler star.

A humbler star with satellites,
Small planets in its train:
And that is why I kneel and kneel
Before Great Chaugnar's fane.

Long is also able to bring poetry into his prose, and the
present volume contains several prose poems of the same high
quality as his verse. The most successful one is perhaps "Felis,"
a celebration of the feline species of which both Long and his
friend Lovecraft were so fond, with the unforgettable ending:

I shall go down, smothered by their embraces, feeling their
warm breath upon my face, gazing into their large eyes, hear-

ing in my ears their soft purring. I shall sink lazily down through oceans of fur, between myriads of claws, clutching innumerable tails and I shall surrender my wretched soul to the selfish and insatiable god of felines.

The book also reprints the contents of *The Eye Above the Mantel & Other Stories* (1995), consisting of the four stories he wrote for the amateur press in the 1920s and 1930s. Of these four, two in particular—"The Eye Above the Mantel" and "In the Tomb of Semenses"—read like extended prose poems, standing as excellent examples of what Long was capable of even at the start of his career.

Scattered throughout the book are a large number of pertinent items by other writers, including poems written by Lovecraft to Long; "The Work of Frank Belknap Long, Jr." by Lovecraft; Donald Sidney-Fryer's introduction to *The Darkling Tide;* a poem by the editor; and a rare, very early review of *The Goblin Tower* by amateur journalist Ernest A. Edkins. Far from padding the book, they provide context and perspective, and it is a great service to the reader to have so much relevant bonus material easily accessible in one place.

The packaging deserves mention as well. Perry M. Grayson has done a tremendous job in making this book as attractive as possible. The layout is clean and airy, and generously sprinkled with photographs (both black-and-white and color) and reproductions of manuscripts. I am excited to see what the future will bring from Tsathoggua Press—it certainly is off to a promising restart after its long hibernation.

No sun is without its spots, and it is only fair to point out the ones that *When Chaugnar Wakes* has. One misattributed poem has snuck in: "Ship of Immortality—A Lament for Strange Tales" comes from a letter from Long to Lovecraft, but is in fact a quotation from *Apollo and the Seaman* by Herbert Trench. And the text could have benefited from another round of proofreading; for example, the line "And never ask" on p. 18 is missing 2 or 3 syllables (correct reading is probably "And never even ask"), and "For the great sons" on p. 33 should clearly be "For thy great sons." But in this digital age this kind of error is easily dealt with, and it is to be hoped that they will be eliminated in future printings.

It is a pity bordering on tragedy that Long did not write more poetry, a mode in which he clearly excelled. But what we do have is a treasure to be cherished forever, and I am not descending into empty superlatives when I say that this will most likely be viewed in hindsight as the most important publication of weird poetry in 2024. It will be an indispensable supplement to *A Sense of Proportion: The Letters of H. P. Lovecraft and Frank Belknap Long,* forthcoming from Hippocampus Press.

At Play in Lovecraftian Fields

Géza A. G. Reilly

EZRA CLAVERIE. *The Shadow out of Providence: A Lovecraftian Metatext.* Published by Tim Hutchings. 2015. 85 pp. $40.00 hc. No ISBN.

Synchronicity is a helluva thing. Years ago I purchased the wonderful solo role-playing game *Thousand Year Old Vampire* by Tim Hutchings, and because I was curious about another of his out-of-print projects, *Weird Fiction*, I signed up for his newsletter. Recently I was idly scrolling through one of Tim's newsletters when I stumbled across a promotion for Ezra Claverie's *The Shadow out of Providence*. The book, a collection of two short stories and a play, was being made available via Tim Hutchings's website, thousandyearoldvampire.com, both in limited hardcover and for free in PDF. Normally I recoil from the artificial scarcity of limited-run books, but Hutchings's deployment of a free PDF of Claverie's collection mollified me, and I decided to take a look. If you, like me, trip easily on Lovecraftian works, textually playful works, and theory-inspired interrogations of texts, then you should order one for yourself as well.

The Shadow out of Providence is a beautifully designed hardcover with no jacket. The text is all Ezra Claverie's, and the illustrations and design are done by Tim Hutchings, Daniel Zettwoch, and Erol Otus. Included with my copy were three small, well-constructed inserts—a bookplate, a postcard, and a clear plastic bookmark depicting an Antarctic research base and the horrors that wait beneath the humans' drill.

All fine and good so far. But what of the text of the book? Well, although I'm not quite convinced Ezra Claverie exists (he certainly seems to, based on web presence, but it remains a possibility that "Ezra" might be a mask for Tim Hutchings), he certainly seems to have a deep and abiding interest in Lovecraft—the titular shadow out of Providence, Rhode Island. This is not to say that Claverie's passion for things Lovecraftian is not an untroubled or easy one. Quite the contrary, the texts in *The Shadow out of Providence* seem to be honest attempts to make Lovecraftian things fit into modern life without dragging along the unpalatable realities of who Lovecraft was as a person and what those realities imply about Lovecraftian stories as a whole.

"Driving to Dunwich," the first of the three pieces in this slim book, is a poignant and haunting story set in an alternate universe where Lovecraft not only survived well into the 1950s but became a happily married writer of great renown. We have seen ideas like these in other places (perhaps most notably in *The Lovecraft Chronicles* by Peter Cannon), but the point of this story is not just to reclaim Lovecraft without all the racism and other unpalatable qualities that get discussed ad nauseum today. Rather, the story focuses on the narrator and his friend, Tim Hutchings, diving into the Quabbin Reservoir to capture footage of the drowned town of Dunwich for one of Hutchings's art installations. In this universe, it seems, "The Dunwich Horror" was used as the basis for the Mercury Theater's infamous, panic-inducing radio play (rather than H. G. Wells's *War of the Worlds*), and several lives were lost in Dunwich as a result. Hutchings's great-grandfather was one of the perpetrators of a lynching during the panic, and Hutchings's art installations are seemingly an attempt to understand that moment and the context of the town out of which those actions blossomed. This is a sad story of generational trauma and the way the truth of events can be buried under cloudy water, out of focus for those who come after and need to learn.

The second piece in *The Shadow out of Providence* is a five-act stage play. *Facts Concerning the Late Eadweard Thurston and His Family* was written by Albert Jermyn, the black half-brother of H. P. Lovecraft (Ezra Claverie explains the history of the author in his scholarly Editor's Foreword). The play itself is a dizzying mashup of more Lovecraftian ideas than I can illuminate here, Shakespeare's *Hamlet*, and the work of political philosopher Frantz Fanon (it wears these influences on its sleeve; the Lovecraft elements are of course obvious, but the play features a Fanon quotation and Walter Benjamin's famous quotation about the Angel of History). The play, complete with its set and costume illustrations, had me alternating between laughing and gaping, gobsmacked at the attempt on display here. Nowhere have the pretensions and odious ideas held by Lovecraft been so skewered with so much care and attention. This is not just textual destruction, however, but textual repurposing, and it is glorious—using the master's tools to dismantle the master's house, as it were, and then using those materials to build a new house altogether.

The third section of Claverie's text is no less charmingly convoluted. Erol Otus provides a foreword in "From the Game Designer," discussing the history of his *Under the Ice* video game series (itself based on a fictional pen-and-paper role-playing game by Sandy Peterson, of real-world *Call of Cthulhu* RPG fame). The most recent entry in the series of games is *Under the Ice: Vostok Dossier*, and it is based on documents found by Ezra Claverie, an Antarctic truth researcher. What follows is those documents: a letter written by George Danforth (of *At the Mountains of Madness*) and a record written in slime on an ancient wall. That latter element, "Beyond the Far Islands," is the story that makes up the bulk of this section.

And what a story it is! The protagonist, who I suspect is an adolescent shoggoth, goes on a journey of self-discovery and terrifying exploration. The whole is almost the inverse of *At the Mountains of Madness* itself, only it is told in a breezy, colloquial manner that gives a feeling as though it would be better presented as a SQUA TRONT!–style EC Comics story from the 1960s. Delightfully silly, sad, and harrowing in turn, "Beyond the Far Islands" is a treat to read, with the only downside being that I'm not quite sure what Claverie (if, again, there is a Claverie) is trying to say in the course of the piece. It is also, sadly, the one place in the book where the art works against the narrative. The last element is a modern human letter that is, perhaps due to my colorblindness, almost impossible to read (the same can be said for a letter by George Danforth that comes just before the main narrative).

Still, the whole of the story, as multi-layered as it is, is richly rewarding. Lovecraft's protagonist famously argued that "whatever they were, they were men" while discussing the Elder Things in *At the Mountains of Madness,* and that sentiment is echoed here by Danforth being quoted in the foreword as having said, "There are no monsters, no aliens in Antarctica, save man." What a subtle and brilliant way to clear the ground so that the reader is open not only to a narrative told from the point of view of a monstrous abomination (just as Lovecraft argued that a story told from a werewolf's point of view would be the only way to write a satisfying modern story of that type), but to a monstrous abomination who is, in fact, nothing more than human in temperament and outlook. I will admit that I preferred the first two pieces in *The Shadow out of Providence* to the last, but that doesn't mean I am going to let anyone pry this strange, unsettling, and all-round weird final offering from my hands.

Overall, *The Shadow out of Providence* is one of the rare successful attempts to play with Lovecraft and Lovecraftian creations without jettisoning the uncomfortable elements arbitrarily and artificially (the recent semi-trend of authors changing the name of "Shub-Niggurath" without engaging with that entity on a deeper level springs to mind). Rather, the text is an intelligent, precise, and incredibly insightful piece of work that functions on the level of pure aesthetic enjoyment, on the level of academic intellectualism, and on the level of pure, fun, insane punk rock remixing. I could not recommend *The Shadow out of Providence* more, and Ezra Claverie, should he exist, deserves to be lauded for this effort. Even if you do not want to burden your shelves with such a slim offering, the text is quite literally free in PDF form on Tim Hutchings's website. What do you have to lose but your chains?

As Worthy a Search as the Searcher

Géza A. G. Reilly

LEIGH BLACKMORE. *Nightmare Logic: Tales of the Macabre, Fantastic, & Cthulhuesque.* Gold Coast, Australia: IFWG Publishing International, 2024. 290 pp. $14.99 tpb. ISBN: 9781922856746.

In his author's afterword, Leigh Blackmore details how the works in his collection *Nightmare Logic* have taken him decades to complete and assemble. I wouldn't have been able to guess the length of time involved while reading; the collection seems ready-made and clean upon a first perusal. The strength of Blackmore's craft is evident throughout, and while *Nightmare Logic* isn't the strongest collection I have ever read, it is certainly a balanced, solid piece of work. Would that Blackmore produced more stories like the highlights in this collection more often!

The twenty-three stories herein are broken down into two broad categories: "Tales of the Macabre and Fantastic" and "Tales of the Cthulhuesque." I must admit that I found myself drawn more to the former than the latter—to my surprise, being an inveterate Lovecraftian myself. Though the first section opens with what I feel is a bit of a dud of a story, "The Sacrifice" (wherein a village is sacrificed to the narrator's Lady Astaroth and an obvious conclusion is reached), it quickly swings into high gear with works like "Imago," a touching story of hope destroyed by circumstance; "By Their Fruits," which in another life I could see Blackmore turning into a classic *Tales from the Crypt* episode; and "Waves," a vignette of a dream of a near-death experience at a beach. From there, the hits (for the most part) keep on coming.

The second section of Cthulhuesque tales, however, struck me as a bit weaker. Most of the offerings here are well written, but they often felt thin in conception to me. "Waiting for Cthulhu," for example, is a short play parody of Samuel Beckett's classic *Waiting for Godot*, and while it is funny, I felt it didn't have much to say. The same is true of "The Music of Erich Zann: A Screenplay," which is, while an able screenplay, just a screenplay adaptation of Lovecraft's eponymous story. Better are "The Horror in the Manuscript" and "The Return of Zoth-Ommog," though I was personally disappointed by both stories, since they hinge on August Derleth's reinterpretation of the philosophical outlook Lovecraft wove into his stories. The best of the bunch in this section is undoubtedly "The Roomer," but even that is marred—albeit slightly—by the inclusion of totally unnecessary explanatory footnotes. If we are very lucky, perhaps Blackmore will write more of this unholy fusion of Lovecraft and Charles Bukowski—if only he would trust his readers to puzzle out local slang through context instead.

What is present in the best of the stories included in *Nightmare Logic* is a sense of desperation and disconnection. Blackmore is at his most poignant and focused when his work centers on those characters who are fundamentally outsiders, divorced from the people and the world that they very much wish to have a connection with. The aforementioned "Imago" is an example of such a tale, but so too is "The Hourglass," wherein a hapless individual gets bound up in mystical horrors that he cannot comprehend while pursuing love. "The Morsels" is a *conte cruel* about a man who is dragged into supernatural terror while attempting to rekindle his passions in life after the unexpected and horrific death of his daughter. And in "Water Runs Uphill," a man mourns the death of his wife while fleeing the very thing that might allow him to move past his loss.

Yet there are still duds here. "The Sacrifice" is not a very strong opening, as I said, and "The Guardian," while a charming reminiscence of Clark Ashton Smith's narratives, is a bit too thin and mechanical for my liking. "The Squats" is a wonderful look at urban living in Australia, but it comes to a neat and obvious conclusion with little thematic support to the imagery it provides. Similarly, "The Last Town" and "Dream Street" are well written, but they are a bit too close to the border of being precious for my liking. To be clear, this is not to say that these stories are bad. Blackmore is in control of his prose, and he deploys it excellently throughout. When he sticks the landing with his conceptions and emotional resonances, he sings. But when one element is off, it's a bit like watching a play with misaligned stage dressing; one can see the mechanisms behind the whole show rather than concentrate on the performance itself.

And then there is the novella "Uncharted." I am not exaggerating when I say that the presence of "Uncharted" makes the collection worth the price of its purchase. Perhaps Blackmore is sick of the praise that this Ditmar-nominated story has gained, but I frankly don't care and will heap more of it upon him. This tale of the protagonist David and his occultist friend Adrian Ash, and how that friendship influences David's intimate relationship with the linguist Svetlana, is simply a masterpiece. There are times when, while listening to music (punk or industrial in my case), one can hear the raw, powerful intention behind the singer's performance; they mean what they say, and the bleeding honesty of it slams into the listener, shaking them down to their bones. That is precisely the experience I had while reading "Uncharted." Blackmore is screaming here, and sighing, and the sense of potential deferred as the monstrous progression of time rolls on is presented in such a way that the universality of it is felt like a dagger in the heart. The ending, which I will not spoil, is terrifying and wonderful all at once, and I can safely say that the novella is easily one of the best things I have read in years.

So we have the heavyweight champion of "Uncharted," beautiful pieces like "Imago," and fun (and often blood-soaked) romps like "Dr. Nadurnian's Golem," "By Their Fruits," and "The Infestation." We have quiet reflections like "Water Runs Uphill," "Waves," and "Leaving Town," and we have standouts like "The Hourglass," "The Roomer," and "Cemetery Rose." Among those is the occasional misfire that lands wrong due to various matters of personal preference. This is not, I think, a sign of an uneven collection. It is, rather, the sign of an author who has struggled for a very long time to figure out what he wants to say and how he wants to say it. What Blackmore has provided us with in *Nightmare Logic* is a record of that search, a map in pieces that leads from the lower initial forays ("The Last Town") through the marveling at the wonders created by those who have come before ("The Horror in the Manuscript," "Beneath the Carapace") and on into the culmination of his search ("Uncharted," "Imago," "The Roomer").

It is as worthy a search as Blackmore is a searcher. I was pleased to follow him on his journey through highs and lows alike, and I found sympathetic vibrations throughout everything he had to say—vibrations that anyone who has felt like an outsider, crushed under the heel of years and expectations, will similarly feel. Now that Blackmore has arrived at his destination and *Nightmare Logic* can rest comfortably on our shelves, one can only hope that he will set out again. And, if we are lucky, he will not take quite so long to find what he is looking for this time.

Emotional Landscapes

David Peak

SIMON STRANTZAS. *Only the Living Are Lost*. New York: Hippocampus Press, 2023. 244 pp. $20.00 tpb. ISBN: 9761614984214.

Weird fiction often feels like a small, crowded field. Perhaps this is because the genre's formal requirements are so narrow, or perhaps it's because its defining characteristics (an emphasis on atmosphere, the hint of supernatural forces, and the suspension of the laws of nature) can be traced back to a handful of names. Either way, it is hard for contemporary weird fiction writers to differentiate themselves. As Michael Cisco writes in *Weird Fiction: A Genre Study*, "The genre of weird fiction is full of redundancy. Select any conventional theme, and there will be dozens if not hundreds of interchangeable stories on that theme, along with the noteworthy ones."[*]

Thankfully, Simon Strantzas frequently writes stories that are noteworthy. Over the course of five collections and two chapbooks, Strantzas's star has risen above that of many of his peers, perhaps most visibly with his 2014 collection *Burnt Black Suns*. Back then, the first season of *True Detective* was a cultural phenomenon. Many people were discovering Robert W. Chambers for the first time. Eugene Thacker's *In the Dust of This Planet* was being discussed on Radiolab. And new and notable anthologies were seemingly being published every month, often stacked with impressive rosters.

The timing was fortunate for Strantzas, and the cover copy for *Burnt Black Suns* was shrewd, taking care to reference both Lovecraft and Chambers. This time around, the cover copy for *Only the Living Are Lost*, Strantzas's sixth collection, emphasizes how his stories have "an emotional resonance that sets them apart from much of the work in this field." Indeed,

---

[*]Michael Cisco, *Weird Fiction: A Genre Study* (London: Palgrave Macmillan, 2021), 4.

this is often lacking in by-the-numbers weird fiction, in which hapless protagonists make stupid decisions and get into bad situations that only get worse. By contrast, the strongest weird fiction tales ground themselves in a complex, emotional reality before twisting things, particularly the drama of messy relationships, the grief of mourning, or the idea that maybe the people we trust most aren't who we think they are. I'm thinking of John Langan's unimpeachable novel *The Fisherman* or stories such as Livia Llewellyn's "At the Edge of Ellensburg" and Laird Barron's "Mysterium Tremendum."

This sort of emotional foundation is something Strantzas has explored before with his 2011 collection *Nightingale Songs*, which includes stories that focus exclusively on relationships. Similar territory is covered in *Only the Living Are Lost*. Sometimes these relationships hint at something larger and unspoken, such as the opener, "The King of Stones." Other times, the details are foregrounded, such as the family drama on display in "Vertices." But always Strantzas takes the time and puts in the work to create that emotional resonance.

In "The King of Stones," two middle-aged women, Judith and Rose, are on a road trip through a remote stretch of Idaho when they decide to pull over and take photographs in a peach-tree orchard. In direct, evocative prose, Strantzas writes:

> Rose's hair caught the sun and wouldn't let it go, a corona enveloping her like a halo. Judith was breathless when she saw it—a deep and sudden remembrance or how much she truly loved her. Despite the irritations and minor disagreements, she was lucky to be with her. Judith was so overwhelmed, she nearly forgot to raise the camera, and when she did the lens captured the waves emanating from Rose like something by Vermeer.

From there, Strantzas explores the nuances of Judith and Rose's differences, as well as the shared truths that unite them, all of which brilliantly underpin their violent undoing. Of equal quality is "First Miranda," a nasty nightmare of a story about Jules, a man who is seemingly confronted by multiple versions of his wife, each of which seeks to enact revenge for an unforgivable crime he cannot recall.

The final story, "Clay Pigeons," is in many ways the dark star of the collection, and one that firmly establishes Strantzas alongside heavyweights such as Barron, Langan, and Llewellyn. The story focuses on Liv and Reno, two outlaw lovers desperate to pull off one last score so they can leave Egypt's Port Said. At one point, Reno admits to Liv that their success would allow him to make right a wrong from his past. Liv takes in this information, thinking:

> I really didn't know what to say. It was . . . *sweet?* Was that the word? I didn't know; sweet wasn't my thing. It's what they called it when you made moon-eyes at a guy, or hung onto his elbow, or whispered stupid things in his ear. Being sweet was talking in a baby voice to your partner, which is why I never had one. Boyfriends were a waste of time and got in the way. And family? Family wasn't much better. My own was a braided rope wrapped around my throat and knotted through an anchor. Even the thought of their cloying neediness dragged me down. I didn't care if I never saw any of them again. Escaping them was escaping insanity.

In "Clay Pigeons," Strantzas pulls together several defining characteristics of the collection to marvelous effect, commanding emotional complexity, craftsmanship, and a more hardboiled voice. It is a story that combines the sweltering desperation of *Casablanca* with the fiery passion of *True Romance*, with Liv and Reno encircled by a slowly closing network of shadowy criminals, all leading to an impossible betrayal.

Despite these successes, the flow of the collection does have some issues. Two stories—"In the Event of Death" and "Black Bequeathments"—are about inheriting things from relatives who have passed away. Unfortunately, the former is much more successful than the latter. And there are also two noir stories—"Circle of Blood" and "Doused by Night"—neither of which worked for me. A few of the other stories feel derivative: "Thea Was First" retreads ideas better explored by the film *It Follows,* and "Antripuu" comes off as a fairly standard monster story, albeit a well-executed one.

Returning once more to Cisco, who writes that contemporary weird fiction, including the work of Strantzas, often "gives characters a sign of doom that is meant actually to absent them from cause and effect. The sign points outside the domain of intelligible action, leaving them helpless to deal with an unaccountable problem."* Many writers are seemingly content to construct these signs of doom, to trap their poor, hapless characters in machines of nefarious design. Strantzas, however, has other aims, namely creating horrors that reveal impossible emotional spaces filled with the ghosts of longing, regret, and delusion.

Perhaps true horror isn't found at the feet of an ancient god or in the snake-like eyes of the monster that lurks inside man, but rather the idea that we are never fully in control of our relationships with others. Perhaps, we realize, we have hurt those we cared most about. Or perhaps we have never seen ourselves for who we truly are. In these moments, Strantzas suggests, strange emotional landscapes may reveal themselves, new worlds of comfort and forgiveness. Only in entering them, in giving ourselves over to realities most appealing, do we become truly lost, never to be found again.

*Weird Fiction: A Genre Study 94.

A Stuart Gordon Afterworld

Michael D. Miller

Suitable Flesh. Directed by Joe Lynch; screenplay by Dennis Paoli; starring Heather Graham, Barbara Crampton, Judah Lewis. RLJE Films, 2023. Based on a story by H. P. Lovecraft.

As far as H. P. Lovecraft adaptations go, "The Thing on the Doorstep" has not been a serious consideration—until now. In a letter to Robert Bloch, Lovecraft referred to this short story as "experimental." The experimental part isn't quite clear, as "Doorstep" is written as a standard first-person narrative confessional, but perhaps the experiment is the horrifying mind-swapping occurring between protagonists or how Lovecraft prevents most readers from ever guessing which character is possessed by whom. This idea is nothing new as Lovecraft used psychic possession as early as *The Case of Charles Dexter Ward*. According to S. T. Joshi, "HPL was so dissatisfied with the story upon its completion that he refused to submit it anywhere." (Later, Lovecraft reluctantly sent it to Farnsworth Wright who published the story in the January issue of *Weird Tales* for 1937).* The story does not rate high in the Lovecraft canon for many critics, but that might be what makes it perfect for a film adaptation.

It doesn't take long to realize what type of adaptation *Suitable Flesh* is—a Stuart Gordon tribute. We have a screenplay by veteran Gordon collaborator Dennis Paoli (skilled in many a Lovecraft adaptation), a lead role for Barbara Crampton (who hasn't aged a year), a cinematic and directing style closely emulating Gordon's vision via Joe Lynch, with sets inside the Miskatonic University Med School designed to look exactly like Gordon's *Re-Animator* (1985). Shot in "cthulhuscope," this is not just an adaptation of Lovecraft's story; it is another

---

*Explanatory note to *The Thing on the Doorstep and Other Weird Stories* (New York: Penguin, 2004), 438.

film in the Gordian Miskatonic Cinematic Universe.

The "Miskatonic Cinematic Universe" roughly refers to the Lovecraft film adaptations made by Stuart Gordon: *Re-Animator, From Beyond, Dagon*, the *Masters of Horror* episode "Dreams in the Witch House," and broadly, any film adaptation by the core filmmakers set in their version of Miskatonic University and Arkham. This version lives in the modern day, minimizing the "Cthulhu Mythos" elements while maximizing the horrific, typically in overexaggerated violence, gore, and sex (often when there are none explicitly in the Lovecraft sources). These films create a mood and atmosphere all their own, making them seem part of a shared universe, and *Suitable Flesh* fits perfectly into that cosmic order.

So what do these Stuart Gordon veterans do with Love-craft's story? "The Thing on the Doorstep" has seven sections; the first five are backstory and exposition, with the last two being the action and climax of the story. Paoli eschews those first five sections and plunges us right into the central plot: an evil entity possessing one mind after another and leaving utter havoc in its wake. First we have some gender-swapping. Edward Pickman Derby is now Dr. Elizabeth Derby (Heather Graham); her husband is "Edward Derby" (Jonathon Schaech); Daniel Upton is Dr. Daniella "Dani" Upton (Barbara Crampton); and Asenath Waite is Asa (Judah Lewis). Ephraim Waite (Bruce Davison) remains the same gender, somewhat preserving the original intent of the vile character. On the surface these choices seem like a gender- (or biological sex-) swapping rodeo. Next, the entire background from the story (and characters) is removed, as well as the "witch-cursed, legend-haunted Arkham" atmosphere, while keeping Miskatonic University front and center. Lastly, the courtship of Edward and Asenath has been removed and replaced with a psychologist/patient relationship between Elizabeth and Asa, with all the "mythos" elements expunged except for one forbidden book, the title of which Ephraim states is "none of your fucking business." What does remain, and perhaps all that matters, is the theme of psychic possession.

Lovecraft treated such a theme as cosmic horror and felt it to be among one of the most fearful possibilities of the unknown. The sense of this is often described in the story as "there swept over me such a swamping wave of sickness and repulsion—such a freezing, petrifying sense of utter alienage and abnormality" or "a cosmic panic and loathing such as only the nether gulfs of nightmare could bring to any sane mind." The film focuses less on cosmic considerations on more on body horror, what the possessing mind is doing with the host body—your body—using it for killing or carnal pleasure with wild abandon. In doing so the film creates stronger bonds with these characters through showing this than Lovecraft ever did in telling us.

In the film narrative of *Suitable Flesh*, Elizabeth is a therapist, looking for a perfect case study to complete her book on out-of-body experiences and schizophrenia. Her newest patient, Asa Waite, is such a case. He complains of being mentally attacked by his father, Ephraim, then right there in the session he receives a phone call from Ephraim, who utters a bunch of sounds through the phone including "Iä fhtagn" and Asa is possessed, kicking the story off into overdrive. Elizabeth takes valiant steps to save Asa, but the spirit of Ephraim jumps bodies, from Asa to Elizabeth to her husband Edward, exploring each body as a new experience and murdering anyone in the way.

Such scenes might be an overload of sleaze and kink, not unlike a soft-porn flick for the premium channels, but this is a Stuart Gordon tribute, lest we forget his origins directing David Mamet's play *Sexual Perversity in Chicago*. Elizabeth calls upon her lifelong friend Dr. Derby, head of the psychiatric ward at Miskatonic U, only to pull her dangerously into the intrigue. This film vibrantly sparks to life when Crampton is on screen ("I have the power to have you committed faster than you can say reasonable doubt"), and the performances of the actors possessed by Ephraim are viscerally convincing. (Do not call them scream queens or Crampton will put six bullets in you faster than Daniel Upton.)

Dealing with the ever-present smartphone in storytelling is always a point of contention, and using them conveniently as an avenue for possession is a weak point. Apparently all one needs to hear is "Iä fhtagn" three times and possession occurs, but Lynch's use of the split-screen technique occasionally to watch the possessor and the possessed unites the tension. We also get tons of Easter eggs from a Lovecraft bust in Elizabeth's office, to Arkham addresses like "33 High Street" and the appearance of a *Dunwich Press*.

Overall, there is not a dull moment in this splatter horror film, all the way to the climactic end. Crampton and Graham are truly believable as best friends, and they show a bond that outlives and outwits the sanity-blasting events pulling them ever apart, celebrating true friendship only glossed over in Lovecraft's story. In unison with the theme, the gender swapping, and Lovecraft updating, they say to us, the future is female.

This film updates Lovecraft without correcting Lovecraft, accepting him as the origin of great stories, many fit for the cinema, while leaving his greater themes intact. This view may not have ultimately bothered Lovecraft, fitting quite well within his own epistolary world. Lovecraft had many correspondences with women, more than we think, and helped many in the development of their writing. While the film pushes certain taboos likely to have upset the "old gentleman," we shouldn't forget that "The Thing on the Doorstep" certainly pushed boundaries for its implicit repressions of gender, identity, and sex. After all, Ephraim, in Asenath's body, is having a sexual relationship with Edward Derby. *Suitable Flesh* pushes these taboos even more, with characters having sex with their bodies while in the mind of another. Again, the film shows what Lovecraft only tells or suggests.

Final words: if you are a fan of "The Thing on the Doorstep" or Lovecraft's fiction, see this film. Even more, if the Miskatonic Cinematic Universe of Stuart Gordon is dear to you, see this film. And if that isn't enough, if you want to be weirded out, freaked out, with heart, see this film. *Suitable Flesh*, a more than suitable Lovecraft adaptation and beyond suitable Stuart Gordon tribute.

Variations on a Dream

Clint Smith

ADAM GOLASKI. *Stone Gods*. N.p.: NO Press, 2024. 193 pp. $18.00 tpb. No ISBN. $10.00 ebook. ISBN: 9798985254532.

Back when Adam Golaski was pursuing his MFA at the University of Montana (he was a graduate-class colleague of novelist Sharma Shields and followed a few years after author Glen Hirshberg), I was only then approaching an academic institution with enough sobriety to be present, bodily, in my classes at their designated times and at their designated locations, and had rather fervently flung my ambitions toward the enterprise of creative writing.

By the advent of this tumultuous chapter, I'd given up subscribing to the pursuit of a conventional career, which included demoralizing myself by devolving into something as provincial as a teacher (a digression: I'm currently in my twenty-first year as a high-school teacher); and similar to the attitude that resulted in my self-induced academic anemia, I possessed no plan for what to do with this ardent, though aimless, literary pursuit. I just wanted to see if I could pull off the trick of getting something, anything, physically published on tangible paper with genuine ink.

Owing to nothing more than bargain-bin petulance, I often behaved defensively during close readings of my own work, combative when it came to whether or not to use a semicolon; but some of this was simply a symptom associated with the suspicion that I'd wasted enough time and was unwilling to waste any more.

But during those early days, and thanks to a lecturer with whom I'd established an artistically kindred rapport and who had supplied supplemental mentoring, I placed myself within close proximity to the literature and experimentations of the Surrealists. My brush with that movement was rather pedestrian as I became acquainted with the usual suspects, Breton, Magritte, Duchamp; in particular, there was an affectionate emphasis on Max Ernst.

I was already equipped with a longstanding affinity for David Lynch (of course *Eraserhead* is *de rigueur*, but more personally consequential were *Blue Velvet*, *Wild at Heart*, and the magnetically meandering narrative of *Twin Peaks*). Breton called surrealism the "disinterested play of thought," wherein traditional narrative form and conventional logic are discarded. There was a sliver of my mental pie chart that responded to (and still responds to) the dreamy lawlessness of Surrealism, yet there was another portion that bypassed what might, in some cases, be perceived as solipsistic whimsy or artistic arbitrariness. Rather, releasing conventional control, I was placed in close connection with reptilian illuminations of the indefinably profound.

Adam Golaski had already acquired a reverential gravity in the fields of horror and weird fiction by the time I initially pursued his work. This would have been about eight years after the release of his repeatedly praised first collection, *Worse Than Myself* (Raw Dog Screaming Press, 2008) and about three years after he had landed a teaching gig at Brown (he is presently a lecturer at Rhode Island School of Design). At the time I noted that Golaski had a knack of taking instances of the ostensibly mundane and augmenting them into something brilliantly discordant. I was reminded then, and again now, of the Dadaist aesthetics. I think too of Werner Herzog's "ecstatic truth": the trinity of fabrication, imagination, and stylization. The confluence of these "ecstatic" tributaries converges in Adam Golaski's third collection, *Stone Gods*.

What follows is not necessarily an examination of Adam Golaski's agility as a Surrealist, but confronting his symbol-driven fiction places me in close proximity to a less-jaded version of myself, a young person captivated by how charged images stimulated inactive compartments of my atrophied imagination. "The image is a pure creation of spirit," wrote Pierre Reverdy. "It cannot be born of a comparison but of the bringing together of two just realities, which are more or less remote, the more distant and just the relationship of these conjoined realities the stronger the image—the more emotive power and poetic reality it will have." The lesson that version of myself learned was that, at some point, it is beneficial to simply let go of overwrought inspection, as to incessantly dissect the symbol is to exsanguinate it.

Stone Gods is divided into two parts (concluded by a circularly suiting Coda), and though there is a tangible difference in the tonality of this partition, it functions as more of a dissolve, with Golaski's return to familiar motifs and symbols operating less like repetition, and more like a crafty employment of double exposure in film—an intentional superimposition where reality is temporarily (and perhaps more thoroughly) compromised.

The initial division of the collection examines themes of guilt and regret, particularly in the story "Holy Ghost," with doses of meted consequence and punishment. "Wild Dogs" is a predatory contemplation of the confining social-scripts and mating-game elimination in realms of both the common and cosmopolitan (and even those engaged in the game's imitation). The stories in the first portion are loosely dedicated to a focus on the body and interpretations of escape—avulsive fixations on corporeal severance, as in "Refrigerator-Drome" (a wink to Cronenberg's *Videodrome* that is lost on neither author or reader).

The final story in the first half is "A Night-Piece ('Yielding Light')," a time-schism hiccup that offers an appropriate segue to the collection's second sequence, which houses a string of themes associated with human habitations and their girders of illusions. "Unfinished Houses" is a temporal, teeter-totter meditation of how the solitary navigation of private passages helps us course-correct our own compunction.

Here, well past the collection's midway point, Golaski successfully smudges the double-agent Adam(s) with narrators individually situated within the undulating tides of their own revisions (additionally, this "doubling" lends itself to a sense of the uncanny). "So strange," says one of his dead-ringer speakers, "the details I chose to modify." An apt passage accentuating themes of place, safety, and perhaps identity itself can be found in "Woods (Marion)": "These were stories from an adult world, encroaching on my world. Encroaching on the woods that frightened me but also were my joy at that age, at a time when I'd just moved to a new neighborhood, just transferred to a new school, and was nostalgic for my last home (was this the beginning of my nostalgia?)"; and in this, Golaski is asking questions about the nature of preoccupation: with making the choice as to whether anesthetize or reconcile the painful present or the painful past.

In what I would categorize as one of the most poignant pieces, "Open Houses" scrutinizes the coping mechanism in our mental manipulation of reflection and time; the story also isolates some of the more pronounced discussions of guilt-ache and, to a certain degree, the pitfalls of domestic and sub-urban banality. "The Wind, The Dust" contains a number of creepy sequences that have been engineered to linger, leaving an unsettling residue as the final eleven words of the story inch-worming their way toward its uncanny conclusion.

What's more, Golaski seems to be addressing his readers with what I would classify as a suspicious, character candor. To clarify, sans spoilers: by the second part of the collection I am left with the sense that, as opposed to offering intra-fiction discourse, the writer himself, through a static-lashed line, is placing a direct-collect call to his audience. "Their arguments aren't real anymore," says one of Adam's Adams. "Just varia-tions on a theme not very original: Adam's failure to earn sat-isfactorily and his reluctance to surrender the activity that keeps him (maybe) from success."

In our august and Enlightened era of 2024, obligatorily mentioning John Gardner will certainly elicit an eye-roll, but his anecdotes prove far more succinct than my chatty prattle (I'm a shitty student, so it's a healthy exercise for me to revisit the rudiments). While literature, cloaked in varying mediums, may contain "a sequence of casually related events," Gardner writes in that oft-quoted text of his, "what carries the reader forward is not plot . . . but some form of rhythmic repetition: a key image or cluster of images . . . a key event or group of events, to which the writer returns repeatedly, then leaves for material that increasingly deepens and redefines the meaning of the vent or events; or some central idea or cluster of ideas. The form lends itself to psychological narrative, imitating the play of the wandering or dreaming mind (especially the mind troubled by one or more traumatic experiences); and most practitioners of this form ... create works with a marked dream-like quality." It requires nothing more than a reciprocal, participatory paralysis to make these stories work.

And this is not to say that Golaski's fiction functions without plot—don't get me wrong, there are stories that are quite conventional—but similar to the medium of poetry itself, Golaski's contract with his readers is based on, and in some ways dependent upon, the skeletal scaffolding of *content* and *structure*. In the architecture of his fiction, what would otherwise be poetic enjambments are employments of the surreal, cadences of the irreal.

The fifteen stories in *Stone Gods* are a radiative preoccupation of sacrifice, loss, grief, and identity; his voice is contemporarily crisp, at times playful, and his style remains sharp as a broken seashell. Many of Golaski's characters possess perceptive lenses contorted by their own nostalgic reflections, their gazes fixed on inflexible effigies in search of significance. The conclusive maxim is that, ultimately, all we have are stories, allegories that suffuse reality until the tangible world is effectively fogged, its lineaments gone to murk.

In Golaski's writing, his audience is repeatedly drawn—sometimes subtly coaxed, other times viciously hauled—across boundaries and reeled over the cliffs of convention. Often unorthodox, Golaski perpetuates his avant-garde undertakings while maintaining accessibility and an admirably dark weirdness.

Owing to an unapologetic obliqueness, it is easy to imagine some of Golaski's stories as challenging. When we read writers, we rarely have insight into their pain. Often that is evident. Yet these interstitial smudges are necessary to maintain some compelling atmosphere of not only mystery, but companionable consolation.

I have stated previously that one of the compartments of innate validation comes in the form of candidly sharing tales of toil: racing against the clock, against failure, in finding time to suture together projects in the face of daily obligations—the Artful-Dodger methods we, as writers, exploit in order to *make* time. The cynosure of being published is, of course, a criterion of progress and a benchmark for industry acclamation, but our courses require channels of calibration, criticism, and conversation. Accolades roll in ebbs and neaps, but the integrity of this intrinsic "thing" endures. "Some kind of supernatural thing," Golaski writes in one of his older stories, "that thing that occasionally [makes] lonely moments profound."

Adam Golaski's *Stone Gods* is a subversive distillation of literary dexterity and allegory, both personal and universal. By the time we notice one of life's anomalies, readers will find that Golaski has already captured it, placed it under a cerebral bell jar, and altered his specimen into something both instructive and alchemically unconventional.

Living and Loving on a Pestilential Planet

Katherine Kerestman

According to our old friend H. P. Lovecraft, "beauty, which is probably the only thing of any basic significance in all the cosmos, ought to be our chief criterion." This dilettante adores beautiful things in general, including the covers, binding, textures, and fonts of books; and, especially, the words, language, poetry, and prose they house. I sometimes even imagine fondling the letters of the alphabet. When well-written, I enjoy words even more than the texts they make up. That is not to say that I do not enjoy fine stories, wise philosophies, strange histories, and archaic lore—only that I require that these be presented in packages that make the reading of them an aesthetic pleasure.

Another weird attribute of my bibliophilic personality is that I luxuriate in learning: I am one of those perpetual students who is intoxicated by ideas. I like new ideas, different ideas, opposing ideas. I seek out questions more than answers. Being a student, I find that learning a new body of knowledge (such as the oeuvre of a writer I have newly discovered) is facilitated by writing an essay (to myself) on the significance and the unique characteristics of that writer or other topic under investigation. Then, having done my homework, I feel better able to discuss literature than say "I liked" or "did not like" a piece, which is the gist of most book club discussions.

Even more, I enjoy the process of analysis, comparison and contrast, distillation, and other processes that make up Thinking. I find erudition downright sexy. Here, therefore, are my ramblings upon the subject of a writer named H. A. Manhood, whom I discovered in the course of my research for a series of anthologies I am editing (creating?) with S. T. Joshi. The first of these are *The Weird Cat* (WordCrafts Press, 2023) and the new *Shunned Houses: An Anthology of Weird Stories,*

Unspeakable Poems, and Impious Essays (WordCrafts Press, 2024). Researching these volumes of forgotten lore has been such a boon in my life: I feel like a literary Nancy Drew shining my flashlight into dank and mildewing literary crawlspaces and sometimes finding lost treasures.

Howard Alfred Manhood (6 May 1904–January 1991) lived in rural Sussex; the fact that he raised his own food there is consistent with the intimate relationship between people and nature he depicts in his fiction. He published one novel, *Gay Agony* (1930), but is better remembered as a prolific short-story writer whose narratives are set in the countryside of England. His stories were published as three collections and in numerous respectable literary magazines. While overtly weird elements may characterize only some of his tales, through choices of diction and deployment of value-laden descriptive details Manhood nearly always hints at the occult or unseen, even in his more realistic stories. *Nightseed and Other Tales* (1928) is a collection of sixteen of Manhood's stories of exceptional power to move the reader.

England is a nation of walkers. The narrators of *Nightseed* are walkers, too, wanderers upon the earth who seem in their roving to meet all manner of people living in a variety of singular situations, or living in common situations viewed with fresh eyes. Although usually well-meaning, his storytellers tend to commit hasty judgments of their fellow men (not meaning to be unkind or superior), later to regret having spoken prematurely. Repeatedly, a deeper understanding of a situation gives Manhood's storytellers cause to repent their haste. Sometimes such errors of judgment yield tragic results.

In "Andrew God-Himself," for instance, the vagabond narrator blames a taciturn husband for depriving his lively and convivial wife of social intercourse and pleasing conversation. When he departs from their home (they have given him a place to stay for a couple of days without asking remuneration), the meddling storyteller uncovers evidence of his host's murder of a rival for his wife's affections; hence the man's sad and reserved aspect. The husband is living with his guilt and with the burden of his wife's betrayal. Once he has learned that their guest has discovered his guilt, he kills himself.

The bride in "Honeymoon," tells her story in the purser's cabin. After embarking upon an Atlantic voyage/wedding trip, she discovers her pastor-husband's unloving complacency toward both herself and their marriage; indeed, as he courts a rich elderly woman, grooming her for a hefty donation to the church, she becomes aware of her husband's cold and calculating attitude respecting human relationships in general. Panicking at her new insight into just what she has gotten herself into, she tells him an outrageous fib (?) about her past sexual misconduct, just to jostle his ghastly complacency. He reacts with rage, calls her a "bitch," and then jumps overboard, preferring death to a tarnished reputation. The bride is as nonplussed as the reader at the extreme nature of her husband's reaction.

Manhood's descriptive prose anthropomorphizes most of the inanimate objects and flora that appear upon his pages, granting them a real agency: they create and participate in the mood or character of the surroundings. The people of his tales are as organic as the plants. Each is an outgrowth of their natural environments; and, although their lives are not wholly determined by their circumstances, they are significantly influenced by them. Manhood's gorgeous sentences are sumptuous and lengthy. Filled with lists of descriptive details relative to both persons and settings, they conjure moods of rich textures, much in the same way that a high thread-count yields a plusher carpet. From the descriptions of the pattern on a fabric to the fluttering of flower petals or the facial expression of a pike, the implications of environmental minutiae build a dense and complex mood. A multi-layered, multi-sensory world is constructed around the reader, and the reader feels himself an active participant in the events described.

Being part of the setting is not always a pleasant experience, though. The little girl of "Misery Cottage" is abused, even put up for sale, by her father; she finally commits murder-suicide through the ingestion of deadly nightshade. Manhood's genius and descriptive power make this sad tale a work of art. The deadly flora, as well as the misery of the father and the child, seem to have grown out from a pestilential planet:

A staring-eyed, sulking place it was, of flint with brick corners, hung with rags of ivy, a perfect beggar among cottages, well deserving of its name. Looked at from the road it seemed to be bending over to gaze at its own reflection in the muck-clouded pond at its feet. The walls bulged everywhere as if it were with child. A basket had been clapped over the central one of the three chimneys—evidently to discourage nesting birds—giving it the appearance of an erring madam under escort. A brass bed-knob glared shrewishly from a curtainless upper window. Upon one side of the crumbling porch was a cracked chamber pot filled with dead ferns, and on the other a twisted snake of piping with a dribbling, blackened tap for a head. The skull of a horse lay upon a lower sill, together with an old boot and half a loaf dried to a chalky hardness. The surrounding garden, tenanted only by a lonely bullace and vagabond mauve and white mallows and dust-heavy nettles, had a disheartened, trampled appearance, vastly unsettling to the soul. A single smudgy duck floated upon the pond, diving under every minute or so as if determined to commit suicide. You could smell misery even if its presence had not been advertised by the chalked copper-lid nailed to the doddered oak by the gate, surely the most disquieting notice ever displayed. Each letter was a firm as a hoof-print, all except the last, which threatened to slip off the board altogether:

FOR SALE
HEALTHY CHILD
PRICE FIFTY POUNDS

—a tragedy sketched in just seven words.

The prose of *Nightseed* is chiefly fashioned of the narrators' stream-of-consciousness recollections of the lives they cross in their travels. Interior monologues dramatize their contemplations, which lead them to new conclusions as they incorporate new data into their thoughts. Manhood's tone is kindly, yet quite serious—even melancholy and solemn. An observer of human nature and experience, Manhood achieves wisdom through the scrutiny of painful experiences; in that empathy and forgiveness are key elements of his tales he is evocative of

Nathaniel Hawthorne. The protagonist of "The Cough" is a writer who is so annoyed by a coughing neighbor (whose cough interferes with his writing) that he contemplates murdering him; he even infects his landlady with the thought of murder. His self-pity is tempered when he meets a poor woman in the street: in that encounter, a seed of compassion for his sick neighbor is sown. Abashed at his selfishness, he visits the sick man armed with cough medicine, and he receives a practical reward for his thoughtfulness: inspiration to write a story about the invalid. He arrives just when the consumptive woman draws her last breath. His discovery that the annoying neighbor, whom he always thought of as a man, is a woman enhances his shame. He also discovers that the landlady has taken a murderous step—and that he has prevented the death of an innocent by visiting the invalid in time to foil the scheme he himself had suggested to her.

Compassion for other-than-human animals, too, is a recurring motif. Manhood does not "personify" fauna; he writes of animals as individual persons in their own right who daily suffer the tragedies of sentient beings routinely treated as objects and regularly subjected to gratuitous suffering for humans' pleasure. In "The Hero," Jacob the Rat, hidden in a soldier's pocket, is sacrificed to make room for loot. The wife of a fisherman is doomed when her tongue is ripped by the hook when her husband casts his line in "The Dainty Pike." Chance, the wayfarer in "Brotherhood," purchases a chaffinch from a woman who tells him that the bird has been blinded by a hot needle to enhance his singing ("They don't feel it at all, y'know," the woman says).

Nightseed, as a whole, is an extended prose poem that forms an appeal to the human capacity to be a higher form of life. Sublime, somber, filled with love, regret, and hope, *Nightseed and Other Stories* is a volume that needs to be reprinted for a hurting world sorely lacking in compassion, forgiveness, and understanding. The man and woman of the title story, "Nightseed," agree that love is the only justification for being, the only thing that is real. They consummate their love and their need for each other in the meadow without shame.

John Martin Leahy and the
Lost Race Adventure Tale

S. T. Joshi

Very little is known of the life of John Martin Leahy (1886–1967), although some facts that may shed light on his work have recently emerged.* Leahy was born on 16 May 1886 in Newcastle, King County, Washington State, the son of Michael Joseph Leahy and Elizabeth Ann "Lizzie" Martin Leahy. John's father was the son of Irish immigrants; his mother's family was from Kentucky; John's middle name Martin was taken from his mother's maiden name. He was the eldest son, and three sisters (Katie, Mary, and Margaret) and two brothers (Irvin and Jim) followed him.

Census data show Leahy as living in Newcastle as a toddler in 1890; by 1910 he is found in Seattle, where he lived with his family; his father was employed at the Northern Pacific Railroad at this time. Curiously, Leahy's own occupation was listed as basket maker. The 1920 census lists his occupation as stenographer; in the 1940 and 1950 censuses his occupation is given as either "writer fiction" [*sic*] or "freelance writer," although by this time Leahy was in fact writing—or, at any rate, publishing—nothing. In 1942 his World War II registration card gives his place of employment as Puget Basket & Package Company in Seattle. Leahy never married. An undated newspaper article by Doug Margerson states that "John became an eccentric and a recluse, living out his life in a cabin on Lake Sammamish, surrounded by books and the watercolors he taught himself to paint."

Leahy published four short stories and three serialized novels, all in *Weird Tales* except for one of the novels. His skills as an artist paid dividends in one instance, as he was the cover artist on the Fantasy Publishing Company's reprint of *Drome*

---

*For many of these details I am deeply indebted to the research of Sunni K Brock.

(1952). But this modest body of work—included in its entirety in this volume—is far above the level of routine pulp fiction.

It may well be the case that Leahy's three novels—*Draconda* (*Weird Tales,* November 1923–May/June/July 1924), *The Living Death* (*Science and Invention,* October 1924–May 1925), and *Drome* (*Weird Tales,* January–May 1927)—are variations on the same basic idea: the notion of a lost race of human or quasi-human beings, either on this planet or on Venus. *Draconda* is in many ways the most interesting of these, at least from a philosophical perspective. Here, the scientist Henry Quainfan has found a way to get to Venus. He is convinced that Venus is inhabited and believes that the surface of the planet is "cool and equable." This was not, at the time, as preposterous as it now sounds. There was much speculation as to the surface conditions of the planet, some astronomers believing that Venus was steamy and swampy like our own Palaeozoic age, others believing that it was a barren desert blown by dust storms; still others thought that the planet was covered with huge oceans of carbonated water or even with hot oil. It was only in 1956 that radio waves showed the surface temperature to be a minimum of 570° Fahrenheit, while in 1968 radar and radio observations at last confirmed the temperature to be 900° Fahrenheit and the surface atmospheric pressure to be at least ninety times that of the earth.

In any event, Quainfan and his friends Rider Farnermain and Morgan St. Cloud undertake the voyage in a vessel called the *Hornet.* Landing on Venus, they find evidence of creatures they are accustomed to seeing on Earth, including the footprints of "a naked human foot." Eventually they come upon an entire civilization of human creatures, led by a beautiful queen named Draconda. Incredibly, she speaks English. How can this be?

Throughout the early parts of the novel, Leahy's characters conduct a philosophical/religious debate over the implications of the existence of an intelligent species on another planet. Farnermain is apparently an orthodox Christian—indeed, one who is somewhat old-fashioned in his views. Quainfan accuses him of believing that "the Universe was made for man." Quainfan himself is a "materialist." The existence of humans (and other creatures known on Earth) on Venus triggers a discussion of the validity of the theory of evolution. Farnermain throws down a gauntlet: "Where now is your evolution? Where now is your Darwinian pipe-dream?" Quainfan is, indeed, initially taken aback; when he sees what appears to be a lion, he bluntly states, "All my evolutionary beliefs are shattered." Later he acknowledges that the "Almighty" placed human beings on both Earth and Venus for some unknown purpose. But this discussion is rendered null and void, and the truth of evolution vindicated, when Draconda ultimately explains (not entirely plausibly) how she did come from Earth, and also how she could be both only twenty-five years old on Venus but a hundred and twenty-five years old on Earth. (Whether her explanation sufficiently accounts for the presence on Venus of the other members of her civilization is not at all clear.)

Religion in Draconda's realm also plays a factor in the novel. When the terrestrial explorers first come upon the people of Venus, they are conducting a barbaric religious rite involving human sacrifice. The explorers break up the ceremony and save a young woman, Mynine, who was about to be killed. But her love for Quainfan turns to hate when he falls in love with Draconda; and Mynine thereafter leads a campaign to overthrow Draconda. The final segments of the novel present an exciting account of the conflict between Draconda's forces and Mynine's (aided by a high-priest, Sallysherib, who also harbors hostility toward the queen). Leahy repeatedly cites the battle of Cannae (in which the Carthaginian general Hannibal, in 216 B.C.E., defeated the Roman army by a pincer movement), as Draconda's forces triumph in the same manner. *Draconda* is the longest of Leahy's three novels and probably the richest in its intellectual underpinnings and dramatic pacing.

The Living Death appeared in Hugo Gernsback's *Science and Invention,* a proto–science fiction magazine that began publication in 1913 under the title *The Electric Experimenter;* in 1920 the title changed to *Science and Invention* (this had previously been the subtitle of the magazine), and it ran under this title until it ceased publication in 1931. It was in fact predominantly a nonfiction magazine, and what fiction it published more focused on scientific gadgetry than Gernsback's *Amazing Stories* (1926f.). *The Living Death* has a quasi-scientific premise in the scientist Darwin Frontenac's invention of a means of restoring life to creatures who are in a state of suspended animation. Whether this can be done with human beings is an untested assumption, but Frontenac has a chance to conduct such an experiment when a colleague, Stanley Livingstone, reports on an expedition to the Antarctic that was undertaken on the belief that "there may be an unknown race somewhere in the heart of Antarctica."

Livingstone is well aware that the climate of the Antarctic continent was once tropical, but he is nonetheless astonished when he and his expedition come upon a realm they call the Gardens of Paradise. But the exploration of this unknown land turns ominous when Livingstone finds one of his party killed—his head severed, and his body nowhere to be seen. Later Livingstone comes upon the body of a beautiful young woman encased in ice. She must be at least 300,000 years old. Can she be alive? Livingstone comes back and, when he hears of Frontenac's invention, implores him to go back to the Antarctic and rescue the ice-encased woman.

Frontenac, along with his colleague Bond McQuestion, do exactly that. Early in the expedition Livingstone himself succumbs to a killer whale. The explorers also encounter hideous harpy-like entities as well as a "huge bear-man." But of course they are successful in bringing back the young woman (whom they dub Sleeping Beauty) and bringing her to life.

Drome takes place, somewhat implausibly, at—or, rather, *under*—Mt. Rainier, where again an entire unknown civilization is found. The scenario is largely identical to that of *Draconda*. In 1858, an expedition to the mountain—the tallest in the continental United States, at more than 14,000 feet—had found evidence of human beings, as well as of some hideous shapeless monster, underneath the mountain. Now, Milton Rhodes recreates the journey, as he learns that a recent death on the mountain appears to confirm the accounts of the earlier expedition. Rhodes and his companion, Bill Carter, find both a lovely young woman and a batlike monster, whom they dub "the angel and the demon." The "angel" proves to be Drorathusa, a priestess of the underground civilization. She and others of her clan lead Rhodes and Carter to their city, Lellolando, which has a population of 15,000 (!). Later they come to the capital, called the Golden City, where they meet Queen Lepraylya. Further adventures ensue, somewhat along the lines of *Draconda*.

By the time *Drome* appeared, Leahy had established a foothold in *Weird Tales* with the short stories "The Voices in the Cliff" (May 1925) and "The Voice of Bills" (October 1926). After *Drome,* Leahy placed "In Amundsen's Tent" (January 1928) and "The Isle of the Fairy Morgana" (February 1928) in the magazine. Like his novels, these stories share some salient characteristics. "The Voices in the Cliff" features a know-it-all detective, Guy Oxford, who manages to explain how he saw the murder of a woman by her husband, who threw her off a cliff, even though Oxford was on a ship 80 miles out at sea. Oxford is insistent that there is nothing supernatural in the overall scenario. Oxford returns in "The Isle of the Fairy Morgana" to pressure another murderer to confess to his crime by an approximately similar means. "The Voice of Bills" is yet another murder tale that suggests the supernatural only to explain it away at the end.

Leahy's most striking short story—and most celebrated work overall—is "In Amundsen's Tent." Again set in the Antarctic, the tale is in essence a warning not to explore the Antarctic any further, lest subsequent explorers meet the fate of Robert Drumgold, whose diary forms the bulk of the text. Drumgold's account tells of an encounter with a nameless and tantalizingly undescribed entity that is suggested to have emerged from outer space; at one point the human protagonists even speculate that the entity is "hibernating." Dogs react with terror and loathing at the entity. Early in the tale Drumgold engages in a kind of cosmic speculation, wondering whether the earth or the universe is really "made for man": "May not there be other beings—yes, even on this very earth of ours—more wonderful—yes, and more terrible too—than he?"

It should be evident from this synopsis that "In Amundsen's

Tent" was at least a partial influence upon Lovecraft's short novel *At the Mountains of Madness,* written in 1931. The premise of both stories is the warning against exploring a realm that harbors unthinkable horrors. The notion of some hibernating alien species is strikingly similar to that of Lovecraft's Old Ones, who are found by human explorers in a state of cryogenic suspended animation in a cave in Antarctica. Lovecraft commented on the story in a letter to August Derleth (13 December 1927—the issue had appeared about a month before its cover date), remarking: "'In Amundsen's Tent' was *the* story of the issue, though the style is poor—as always with Leahy." That last comment makes clear that Lovecraft read Leahy's previous work in *Weird Tales,* although it is not clear that he read *The Living Death,* also set in Antarctica.

Certain crudities or deficiencies in Leahy's narrative might have inspired Lovecraft to see if he could do better. In particular, Leahy's story ends up being something of a tease, in that he refuses to describe the entity in the tent in any way aside from suggesting its extraterrestrial origin. Lovecraft, in the early stages of his quasi-science fiction phase, made sure to depict the Old Ones with meticulous precision. He avoids any sense of anticlimax in this clinical description because he withholds the true horror of the story—the protoplasmic shoggoth—until the end. And of course Lovecraft vastly expands on the cosmic implications of his narrative, supplying a detailed account of the origin of the Old Ones in the remotest reaches of the galaxy, their advent to earth, and their battles with other alien races, such as the "Cthulhu spawn" and the fungi from Yuggoth (from "The Whisperer in Darkness").

After his story in the February 1928 issue of *Weird Tales,* Leahy fell silent literarily. Why this was the case—he was only in his early forties at this time—is unknown. He did do the cover art for *Drome* when it was published in book form in 1952 by the Fantasy Publishing Co., but that is the last we hear of him. His two other serialized novels have not been reissued in print until recently;[*] aside from "In Amundsen's

---

[*] I have reprinted Leahy's novels and tales in two editions from Sarnath Press: *Draconda and Others* and *The Living Death and Drome* (both 2024).

Tent," which has been reprinted on numerous occasions, his short stories are also little-known.

Leahy was certainly above average as a writer for the pulp magazines, in spite of certain annoying stylistic tics (most notably his use of such affected archaisms as "'twas," "forsooth," and so on) and a generally hysterical and flamboyant style that seeks to wring as much tension out of a given situation or episode as possible. But there is no question that his novels and tales are entertaining and even at times thought-provoking, and that is enough to justify their resurrection.

Some Bodies:
Words about Allison V. Harding,
"The Underbody," and Such

Alex Houstoun

These are some things I know to be true about the works of
Allison V. Harding.

From 1943 to 1951 *Weird Tales* published thirty-six stories
by Allison V. Harding, making her one of the most prolific
writers for the magazine during Dorothy McIlwraith's tenure
as editor. Of these, it seems reasonable to say that Harding
was perhaps best known for three stories featuring the "Damp
Man": "The Damp Man" (July 1947), "The Damp Man Returns" (September 1947), and "The Damp Man Again" (May
1949). In addition to "The Damp Man Again," Harding's stories "The Place with Many Windows" (May 1947), "City of
Lost People" (May 1948), "Four from Jehlam" (January
1949), and "The Underbody" (November 1949) were all the
featured cover stories for their respective issues of *Weird Tales*.

Harding does not appear to have published any work outside of *Weird Tales* and seemingly stopped writing entirely following the publication of "Scope" (*Weird Tales*, January
1951). In fact, Harding's work did not see publication again
until Marvin Kaye's 1988 anthology *Weird Tales: The Magazine That Never Dies* (Nelson Doubleday), in which "The
Damp Man" was republished. In 2020, Armchair Fiction, a
subsidiary of Sinister Cinema Video, released the paperback
collection *Allison V. Harding: The Forgotten Queen of Horror*,
featuring sixteen of Harding's stories. The jacket copy boasts
that this collection is "the first published collection of Allison
V. Harding's works, but it certainly won't be the last." No
subsequent collections have been published.

These are some things that I take to be true about the per-
son(s) behind the name "Allison V. Harding" and some other
things I know to be speculation:

In an ongoing series of articles ranging from 2011 to 2022, Terence E. Hanley, author of the *Tellers of Weird Tales* blog, gathered evidence and developed a theory that has evolved over the years but primarily asserts that Allison V. Harding was a pseudonym and that the real people associated with the name are Jean Milligan (1919–2004) and Lamont Buchanan (1919–2015).

Hanley started *Tellers of Weird Tales* in 2011 shortly after reading "The Damp Man" for the first time, thanks to the aforementioned Kaye anthology. In his second article, Hanley wrote about Harding and the fact that, according to "*Weird Tales* aficionado Robert Weinberg, she was an attorney in New York City" ("Allison V. Harding (?–?)," *Tellers of Weird Tales*, 26 April 2011). It is a short piece and Hanley closes saying, "I have found a couple of newspaper articles about a New Yorker named Jean Milligan, but nothing to tie the subject of the articles to the author of stories for *Weird Tales*. If anyone has information on Allison V. Harding or Jean Milligan, please send it my way."

A month later in May 2011, Hanley wrote a piece confirming the existence of a Jean Milligan of New Canaan, Connecticut, who, in 1952, married a Charles Lamont Buchanan, a prolific writer who served as an associate editor and art director at *Weird Tales* from 1942 to 1949. Hanley also added that per "science fiction historian and editor Sam Moskowitz (1920–1997), Jean Milligan was an attorney in New York City during the 1940s. Apparently that's all he or anyone else knew of her (or at least the people who were telling). Moskowitz evidently based that knowledge on his examination of the files of *Weird Tales* magazine, then in the possession of Leo Margulies (1900–1975), longtime editor and publisher of science fiction, fantasy, and horror." ("Who Was Allison V. Harding?", *Tellers of Weird Tales*, 24 May 2011.)

In an article from 2022, Hanley reported that Moskowitz had opportunity to study the original files and records of *Weird Tales* and, in doing so, discovered that payment for the Harding stories was being sent to Jean Milligan at an attorney's office in New York (*Tellers of Weird Tales*, 29 September 2022). This is where the belief that Milligan was an attorney seems to first originate from. It is not entirely clear when Moskowitz reviewed these files, but it is believed to have been sometime in the 1960s or maybe early 1970s when they were in the possession of Margulies. What is known is that, when *Weird Tales* was sold to Weinberg in the mid/late 1970s, the original files had been destroyed as they had become damaged and infected with insects while being stored in Margulies' garage . . .

On 26 April 2021, the tenth anniversary of his first piece about Harding, Hanley wrote about how it was the Harding mystery that first inspired him to start his blog and that he solved the mystery within a month. He is particularly emphatic and states that "I have to reassert, too, that I am the person who discovered the identity of Allison V. Harding and Jean Milligan. No one else did that, and no one else should be taking credit for the discovery or pretending like it's something that just fell out of the sky. (This is where the passive voice, mostly a scourge, comes in handy. In using it, you don't have to say that somebody did something, only that something happened, no doer necessary.) Anyway, I did it. I discovered the identity of Allison V. Harding. It's my work. I expect to be cited for it." ("A Season of Discovery and Beginning," *Tellers of Weird Tales*, 26 April 2021.) Please note that I am extensively citing you, Mr. Hanley.

Hanley also notes in this retrospective piece that there "has been some controversy recently about Allison V. Harding and Jean Milligan" that he, Hanley, "might have been a little responsible for." The controversy in question is that Hanley had posited that Buchanan was actually the author of most, if not all, of Harding's stories. A little over a year later, on 29 September 2022, Hanley wrote: "I have speculated that Lamont Buchanan was the real author of the Harding stories. I'm willing to consider that he and his future wife worked on at least some of the stories together, in other words that they were co-authors. And I'm willing to consider that everything is as it appears on the surface: Jean Milligan was Allison V. Harding. But that would mean dismissing my feelings and intuition in my reading of the Harding stories."

To summarize, there is no Allison V. Harding but there

was a Jean Milligan and Lamont Buchanan. Stories were published under the Harding name from 1943 to 1951. Buchanan worked at *Weird Tales* from 1942 to 1949. Payment for Harding's stories were addressed to Milligan and mailed to a law office in New York. Milligan and Buchanan married in 1952.

Hanley's "feelings and intuition" about Buchanan being the true other of the Harding stories hinge on the fact that "at least two of the Harding stories—'The Damp Man Again' and 'Take the Z Train'—seem to issue from the male psyche and not at all from the female." According to Hanley, a woman "may be able to approximate what a man thinks, but the author of ['The Damp Man Again'] seems to have had firsthand knowledge of a man's state of mind, of a sick man's cruelty, misogyny, and warped, sick, and twisted thinking in regards to women. I believe the author of that story didn't just imagine The Damp Man's state of mind—he actually lived it, even if only for moments at a time." ("The Strange Case of Allison V. Harding," *Tellers of Weird Tales*, 29 September 2022.) As best as I can read it, Hanley seems to have a hard time believing that a woman in the 1940s and 1950s might be able to have firsthand knowledge of a man's "cruelty, misogyny, and warped, sick, and twisted thinking in regards to women" . . .

Since "The Strange Case of Allison V. Harding," Hanley has written two pieces about Harding. One, "Takings and Turnings" from 4 October 2022, is a bizarre transphobic rambling about how people like J. K. Rowling are being silenced for voicing their bigoted opinions and how "we" have given up on God. Hanley's final piece on Harding, "Allison V. Harding in Tellers of Weird Tales," was published on 6 October 2022 and is essentially a summary of Hanley's entire journey over the past eleven years with Harding, Milligan, and Buchanan. In the final paragraph of the piece Hanley writes: "I think I understand something about the strange case of Lamont Buchanan, who is, I believe, really at the heart of the Allison V. Harding story."

These are some things that I know about myself that eventually explain why you are reading these words:

On 25 April 2009, I went to Brooklyn, N.Y., for my second or third time as an adult. I was traveling with my college roommate/good friend as his band, Nude Beach, was playing a show, opening for a band we were both fond of, Ringers. The show was at Lost & Found, a bar in Greenpoint on the corner of Franklin and Greenpoint. Also playing that show were Stupid Party and Mike Hunchback + The Weird Fantasy Band.

At some point in the evening I started talking with Mike Hunchback. It probably had to do with the fact he was wearing a T-shirt that read "Horton Hears Cthulhu" and was giving away copies of a zine called *Weird Fiction Review* with cover art in a style similar to Lee Brown Coye. According to an email I wrote to Mike the next day, "we talked for a bit about lovecraft [*sic*] and how awesome weird fiction is along with how difficult it is to write." I am going to have to treat the email as fact as I had turned twenty-one the month prior, my roommate at the time was not twenty-one, and he gave me all his drink tickets for the night and I had a lot of fun with drinking for free.

On the morning of 26 April I woke up on the floor, or perhaps the couch, of my roommate's bandmate and, after getting some bagels, we began to drive home. At some point on the Brooklyn-Queens Expressway I started reading the copy of *Weird Fiction Review* I had received. Within the zine is a scanned copy of Harding's "The Underbody" complete with illustrations by Matt Fox as it originally appeared in the November 1949 issue of *Weird Tales*.

I am not trying very hard, but I am trying to convey a little bit about this moment and how it will ripple out over the next fifteen years of my life.

I am young and excitable and kind of dumb because I am junior in college and see a world of potential in front of me and am particularly enamored with pulp fiction and the DIY nature of punk and alternative cultures. I am a little bit hung over and sore and tired, but I also think that this is what it means to be living and taking part in something bigger than myself—yelling along to a band you love and talking to a stranger about the art that inspires you.

There is in my mind a moment where the car I am in is at an elevated turn on the BQE and I am racing toward the conclusion of "The Underbody" and I know what is coming but also I am holding out hope that I am wrong and I am starting to feel a deeper chill of dread. When I finish the story, I roll down my window and stick my head out of the car for a little bit to get fresh air and see if the sun will warm me up some. In the email I write to Mike that evening I include the statement: "you were totally right, the clark ashton smith short was incredible . . . although i gotta say i liked allison harding a whole lot more." (I was young and doing an obnoxious thing where I ignored punctuation in my personal correspondences. I am embarrassed.)

On 27 December 2010 I write an email to Mike saying, among other things "that I really really really loved Allison V. Harding's tale, 'The Underbody'. I was wondering . . . if you happened to have any other works of Ms. Harding in particular." Mike, in his response from the same day, wrote:

> Ms. Allison Harding might not be a Ms. actually, there is some male usage of the name; particularly from Scottish heritage. And I think that "Harding" may be a Scottish name. In his book "The Weird Tales Story" author Robert Weinberg refers to Harding as a "he" but offers no biographical information, only his own distaste for Harding's writing. Weinberg was in his early 20s (mid maybe?) when he wrote that and I personally think that hasty move has led to a MASSIVE ignorance of Harding's writings. In the Weird Tales years that Harding was published s/he was one of their most popular writers (I'm judging by the # of cover stories Harding had) but you'd never be able to tell from the reprint anthologies as I've seriously not seen ONE paperback reprint of anything by her/him. Some other VAUGE leads I've uncovered do say that Harding was a woman, and perhaps a lawyer in New York.

In an email the next day he added, "Ah, yes I had come across the name Jean Milligan also."

My correspondence with Mike continued intermittently for about another year and we would periodically bump into each other at shows. I would last see him at NecronomiCon Providence in 2015 where he was presenting on his book *Pulp Macabre: The Art of Lee Brown Cole's Final and Darkest Era* (Feral

House, 2015).

"The Underbody" is a story that is always kicking around in the back of my mind, particularly when the spring turns to summer or any time I am digging about in a garden.

There is something about the mystique of Harding as a person—and Milligan and Buchanan when you get to it—and the somewhat difficulty of accessing the story online that I find rather appealing. Yes, it is now collected in an anthology that you can buy on Amazon, and yes, it is pretty easy to find Hansley's articles if you search for "Allison V. Harding," but finding the text, the body, of "The Underbody" remains a little tricky. There is also a scan of the *Weird Tales* issue available on the Internet Archive but that, again, requires a particular sort of focused and informed searching that not everyone is inclined to be capable of.

In the fall of 2023 I started a Substack—basically a blog in the form of emails—to send friends and families what I deemed to be "spooky stories." This stemmed from my previously making zines that I mailed to folks with our holiday cards featuring seasonally appropriate ghost stories. When I had started that "project" I found myself looking for excuses and ways to send people stories that fit with other times of the year and, ultimately, rather than making zines sporadically when inspiration struck, I decided that a regular blog/emailing service may be more fitting—spookyseason.substack.com. After registering a name, the first thing I did was see if I could find "The Underbody" online.

The only thing my searching turned up was the Internet Archive scan, which led me to transcribing the story from a PDF scan to a text file so that, maybe someday when it felt seasonally spooky, I could publish the story online.

I haven't done that yet and am now unsure if I ever will.

I have grown attached to the strange journey I have taken with Harding and "The Underbody," as it becomes increasingly harder these days to find weird gaps in knowledge or complete unknowns. For example, I was a little surprised to see how easy it was to fact-check and reconstruct my own recollection of events and the timing simply by going through my old emails and revisiting defunct websites. Sometimes it is fun when things are difficult and unclear, you know?

I have said a lot and not said that much either and it is just about time for me to stop.

I hope you enjoy the following tale. As *Weird Tales* put it, "The country fields of summer hid, within their rich earth, a terror-rid doom to transcend men's ability to fear."

The Underbody

Allison V. Harding

There was a soft summer rain which meant "Stay inside," but with Mother away visiting, Jamie had run out the back door—Father was in the library reading and Cook was in the kitchen baking—across the lawn and down the path that ran into the meadow.

Dr. Holland sat in his favorite leather easy chair in the library, half reading but more interested in looking out the window. It was warm enough to be in shirt sleeves; he was glad that there seemed to be no patients who would need his attention that afternoon, for like the sparrows outside he felt a reluctance to move in the heat and humidity.

There was no sound except the soft hiss of the rain as it touched the griddle-hot earth still overheated from the morning's blazing sun. No other sound except the occasional happy noise of Amanda in the kitchen whipping up cake batter. Amanda was one of those country prizes found in small towns. She filled in when needed and did just what had to be done, as on this occasion, for instance, when Albert Holland's wife had gone across the state for a two-week visit with her own folks.

It was nice to sit here like this not doing anything—the medical journal in his hand had an interesting article, but he didn't have to read it this afternoon. He wondered idly what kind of cake Amanda was whipping up, he hoped it would be one of those thick white ones with chocolate icing and jelly fill.

And it was just then that he heard Jamie yipping and hollering, the sound of his small-boy voice coming from outside, getting louder as the little legs drove him closer.

Jamie had a secret. It was the biggest secret he'd ever had. Too big for its excitement to be contained in his small body dressed garishly in last Christmas' cowboy suit. After looking and looking to be sure, he ran away from it through the field and up the meadow hill, over the stone wall and across the lawn, his little feet splattering through puddles. He started to call before he reached the house, and his father met him at the back door.

"Young man, come in here directly and wipe your feet!"

"Daddy!" gasped Jamie, all out of breath.

His father marched into the library. "You know perfectly well, Jamie, you wouldn't have been out playing cowboy and Indian in this rain if your mother hadn't just gone away!"

"Daddy—"

"Young man, it won't look good for either of us if when Mother gets back, you're sniffling around with a head cold. I think you'd better go upstairs and change. Let me feel those shoes and socks."

"But, Daddy! *Daddy . . . !*"

"Yup, they're wet! Now march yourself upstairs."

"But there's a *man* out there in the field, Daddy, lying all in the ground looking up at me!"

"Now don't you try and get me in on your Indian games, Jamie."

"Really, Daddy, hones' and truly—come an' see!" The little boy's voice rose to a crescendo and he pulled at his father's hand.

"You take yourself upstairs, young man, and change out of that costume. If you want to put on rubbers and a slicker, I'll walk out there with you. What did you say this was . . . an Indian chief?"

"It's no Indian chief, Daddy. Just a man lying there in a hole in the ground!"

"If you want me to go outside with you and help you hunt Buffalo Bill, you go upstairs and do as I told you!"

The little boy clattered away. A few moments later, father and son walked across the lawn over the stone fence and into the fields beyond. The drizzle was over, but mist had taken its place and clung with gray fingers to the meadow.

"Don't tug so, Jamie. Anyway we want to sneak up kind of careful like! I don't want an arrow through me, partner!"

Jamie's excitement increased as they reached the far side of the meadow. There between a boulder and a tree stump he stopped, he looked at the ground and then he looked up at his father crestfallen.

"Mister Mole was there, Daddy, right there!" He pointed.

There was some newly turned earth here, the top of it muddy from the rain, as though Jamie himself or someone else had used a spade. Dr. Holland poked at it with the tip of his boot. There was nothing.

"Guess the Injuns got to him before we could, Jamie. Or maybe a mountain lion got him!"

"He *was* right there, Daddy!"

The physician laughed and put an arm around his son.

"Back to the house with you, youngster."

He liked the boy being imaginative. To him it signaled brains, and that in one's progeny never displeases a parent.

That evening at supper Jamie seemed unusually quiet, and Dr. Holland wondered if he'd made enough of the episode. To please his son he brought it up again.

"Why did you call that varmint Mister Mole, Jamie?"

"Because he was in the ground—stuck in the ground kind of, Daddy."

In the mornings the physician contrived to get their breakfast.

"I'm not much of a cook, Helen," he had confided to his wife, but she laughed and said, "Well, you men can't starve with Amanda getting two meals!"

Later this particular morning the schedule called for him to pick up Cook and she would spin her magic in the kitchen.

Dr. Holland was having a poor time with the breakfast dishes when Jamie came tearing into the kitchen.

"It's Mister Mole agin!" In one great gush of air.

"Jamie . . . now look, you've tracked dirt in here. I don't mind, but you know your mother's told you not to do that and it means Amanda will have to clear it up. Maybe *we'd* better."

"Quick, Daddy!" The little boy was already pulling at Dr. Holland's apron.

"Quick, before Mister Mole goes away!"

The Doctor went, something less than willingly, but forced along by his little son's urgency, out the back door again and across the lawn. And much nearer the house this time, just over the stone wall was a hole—funny, he'd not noticed that before; his son was getting to be quite the boy with the shovel—and in it. . . . Dr. Holland stopped so abruptly that his hand in Jamie's pulled the little boy off balance backward.

"See, Daddy! See, it's Mister Mole, like I told you!"

There were two steps to be taken to the hole in the ground and Dr. Holland took them, instinctively pushing his son back a bit as he did.

The thing in the hole was . . . a man . . . or had been! He was dressed in nondescript brown jacket, shirt and trousers, shoes, and his skin had something of the color of earth too, and there was earth coming from his nostrils and his ears and at the corner of his mouth.

His eyes were opened staring upward—for he was lying on his back—as Holland knelt beside the thing, her noticed the quirk of the lips. The man, whoever he was, could not have been very pretty in life, and the leer turned the face into a distasteful grimace.

The Doctor reached for the wrist. As he lifted it to feel at the pulse, earth fell away from between the fingers. It was as he expected—no beat. He slipped a hand in under the man's jacket and felt over the heart region. There was not the slightest vibration.

He rose, and herding his son before him, hurried back to the house.

"You see, Daddy, I told you about Mister Mole! He comes out of the earth!"

"Now, son, I've got some things to do and I want you to stay here."

So there *had* been someone yesterday! Jamie must have become confused and led his father in the wrong direction.

Holland was due soon for a call on Mrs. Foster, whose nagging arthritis and irritable temperament demanded punctilious attendance by her physician. He thought of calling Ed Quinlan the next house away. Quinlan, aside from being town clerk, was also deputy sheriff of the district; but instead, professional curiosity made Holland first reach for his small medical bag and head out again to that grave across the lawn, unraveling his stethoscope as he went.

He was quite sure . . . well, positively sure, that the man

was dead. The shock of the whole thing—his son, of course, didn't realize the dreadful significance of this gruesome business. He walked briskly—he figured afterward he could not been in the house more than five minutes, and yet . . . yet when he returned and stood there where the spot was, the thing, Mr. Mole, was gone!

"Impossible!" Holland murmured half to himself.

This was the place, no mistake about that. The loose earth; he sifted it with his fingers. There was nothing! *Nothing!* He stood from kneeling and looked around, half fearful that he would find this man he had thought—no, he was sure—was dead walking somewhere away from his earthy grave. There was no one, and he could see a good ways in every direction!

He folded his stethoscope thoughtfully and returned to the house. It came to him that this might be some sort of outrageous joke played by persons unknown, like the time some of the high-schoolers had monkeyed with the pipe on his birdbath and a fire-hose stream of water had come out instead of the usual graceful spray the birds welcomed.

But still it *had* been a body and it *had* been dead. That would mean either grave-robbing or a corpse from some morgue or hospital laboratory.

He instructed Jamie to stay indoors "positively, and don't you dare disobey me" until he got back.

He made his call to Mrs. Foster as short as possible, picked up Amanda and drove back at a great rate to find his son unconcernedly plaything with his toy soldiers on the library floor.

Once, twice during the day the Doctor walked out to the plot of loose earth beyond the wall. Once he went out into the fields where Jamie had taken him the previous day. There was nothing to be seen except what looked like an area of spaded earth.

No more was said until that evening when Jamie brought the subject up just before being ordered to bed.

"Where does Mr. Mole go, Daddy?"

That was a stickler! If you presumed Mr. Mole existed, he couldn't just vanish without reason and to places unknown. If you presumed Mr. Mole didn't exist, then Dr. Holland should instantly fetch his son to an eye doctor and get himself to a psychiatrist!

For several days Dr. Holland thought a lot as he went about his doctor's tasks and as he puttered around the house being a father, and he found more than a few excuses to walk around the lawn and across the stone fence into the meadows beyond.

In a few days the holes where Mr. Mole had appeared lost their freshness, lost their appearance of having been newly turned and again were claimed by the broad bosom of the earth.

It was one evening just before bedtime that Jamie said, "Mister Mole invited me to go for a walk today, Daddy!"

Holland almost dropped his pipe cleaner. He tried to keep his voice steady, for in the silence that had surrounded this subject for several days, it was as though that ugly dream had been swallowed up. The physician kept his voice even with an effort.

"Where was he, Jamie? Where was Mister Mole?"

The little boy indicated with a vague sweep of his arm and repeated again, "He asked me to take a walk with him. Down below, he said, Daddy."

"Jamie!" This thing had gone far enough. "I want you to tell me, when did you first see Mister Mole?"

"The time I told you. That rainy day."

"And, Jamie . . . hones' Injun, now . . . he *talks* to you!"

"Sure, Daddy"

Holland rose to his feet. Something now would have to be done. This could be set upon or dismissed with the hopeful conclusion that it was, after all, only a figment of the imagination.

"Let's go see Mister Mole, son, right now."

"But you can't! He's gone! He went right while I looked!"

"Which way? We'll follow him."

The boy crinkled up his brow as though even to his young and credulous mind, the event was unusual.

"He just kind of went. Down into the earth like. He said he'd be back."

The physician got his son to tell him the whereabouts of

Mr. Mole's latest appearance and then bustled the six-year-old off to bed. He looked for himself later, and there about where his son had described it were the markings of freshly troubled and tossed earth. Precisely what to do was perplexing. His ordered scientific mind made Dr. Holland seek some definite, logical action, and yet there was none.

The thing—whatever it was, and it appeared to be a man—should be examined by the authorities. The first step in that program though, was to find Mr. Mole and constrain him from any more of his vanishings.

Albert Holland spent twenty-four hours thinking over a course of action and then the thought came to him that he should talk to his neighbor, Ed Quinlan, the deputy sheriff who lived across the long meadow that ran out back and down the hill apiece. Quinlan, a widower with a son about Jamie's age, was a nice fellow. He'd always appreciated that Holland had treated him without mention of a bill when things had been tough for the Quinlan's a while back. And he showed his appreciation. But more, he was a bluff, realistic individual whose long suit was not imagination—though he was not stupid by any means—and would, therefore, bring a good slant to bear on this proposition, plus the weight of his official office in the county.

Holland was going to stroll over there this very evening, and now with Jamie bedded down, he was about to start when the knocker of his own front door sounded. It was, coincidentally, Quinlan.

"Hello, Ed!" the physician greeted warmly.

"Evenin', Doc. Sorry to bother you."

"Not at all. Come on in."

Holland saw immediately that the man was agitated. His broad, ruddy face looked worried and his big thick-fingered hands gripped at the somewhat worn Panama he was never without.

"Missus still away, Doc?"

"Yup, another week, Ed."

They talked of things like this and that for some moments and then Ed got around to the point.

"Doc, if your youngster's safe in bed, I wonder if you

could walk down toward my place apiece. Something funny has happened."

Holland waited, his own feeling of uncomfortableness increasing.

"My son, Eddie, Doc. Damndest thing you ever know. He came across a body lying out there—in the meadow back of our place. I thought the youngster was pulling my leg . . . you know the way these kids carry on. Kept after me all afternoon, he did. I went out with him just now, Doc. Seen *him* for myself, I did. All stained from the earth, kind of grinning like. Was the spookiest lookin' fellow you ever saw, Doc. I felt of him myself. Didn't have no more warmth anymore than a tree. Sure he *looked* dead, although I can't really say if there's been some crime committed."

Quinlan stopped and took a deep breath, fiddled with his hat and then fixed his troubled eyes on the doctor again.

"Would you come along with me?"

"Why sure, Ed."

Quinlan hurried on: "I think I saw the fellow move. It was getting kind of twilight out there. I'd sent Eddie back to the house for a flashlight. To be honest, I couldn't see so good. But, Doc, he'd been lying on his back with the earth and all coming out of his mouth like, and when I looked again, I could swear he'd kind of rolled over. But there was still this grin on his face like he'd died smiling—only it wasn't a nice smile—or if he wasn't all dead, he was enjoying this."

The man rattled on, following the physician out into the hall as Holland went to the coat closet to get his own flashlight.

"I'll go with you, Ed."

"But here's the thing, Doc." Ed's hand held him just inside the front door as they were about to step out into the darkness of the summer evening. "I lost him. I must've been watching through the gloom for Eddie to come back with the light and all, but I turned around and he was gone—just like that as though he'd never been there 'cept that I knew he had 'cause the earth was all turned up new-grave like!"

The two walked then, the bobbing flashlight held in Holland's hand showing the way across the lush July countryside.

The night with them and silence now between them; this lawman and the man of science, each with his thoughts and his puzzlement until they stood together, close together, brought there by Quinlan's sense of direction and the bobbing shaft of light that followed to its goal.

Ed's voice sounded small under the black archway of night as he breathed out and said, "There's where he was. Right there, Doc."

And Albert Holland stood and looked at the ground, the familiar look to it. Stood with flashlight beam steady, for there was nothing to do. They both were thinking what to do next and there was no need to say it. Finally Quinlan spoke.

"Guess you think I'm crazy, Doc."

And at that, the physician put his hand on the other's arm.

"No, I don't, Ed. You're not crazy. You saw something." And he was going to say, I saw it too, Ed. Out here in the meadow and then back nearer my house. Jamie called me just as Eddie called you. We've seen *something* all right—in God's heaven just what, I don't know and I'm a doctor and supposed to know what life and death look like.

But he didn't say it because Quinlan was talking some more:

". . . claims he talked to him—imagine this, Doc, a corpse speaking to him—and invited Eddie to take a walk with him, although he couldn't be a corpse moving over onto his side, could he? People can't do things like that—if they're really dead, Doc, can they?" The deputy sheriff was plaintive.

Holland put his arm on the other's shoulder again, this time with more urgency.

"Ed, you say you shooed Eddie home before you came to my place?"

"Why, sure . . . sure!"

Then the two almost automatically started walking towards Quinlan's small cottage just over the brow of the hill, and as they walked, though nothing more was said, their steps speeded.

It was the night that did it, Holland told himself, the night that puts fear into even the most unsuperstitious man, the most prosaic, the most unimaginative, but by rights they *should* feel that way, for this experience the two fathers shared with their two small sons was—poor weak word—extraordinary!

There was a light on the ground floor of the Quinlan house and they could see it through the gloom and it grew bigger as they walked hurriedly towards it. Quinlan, a tightness in his voice now, called as they went forward.

"Eddie! Eddie, lad? Are you there? It's your dad!"

And from the bigger bulk of house ahead of them through the night the small boy's voice came back.

"Gee, Pop, is that you? You been out there in the meadow talkin' to *him?*"

There was no need to answer. Almost simultaneously, their hurrying steps slowed. The crisis, not declared between the two men but appreciated by both of them, was over. Quinlan turned to face the physician.

"Thanks, Doc. Thanks a lot for coming over."

In the dark the two men shook hands. Fervently, it seemed. And then they parted to go their separate ways in the darkness—Quinlan to his home and Dr. Holland back across the night-grown meadow.

Holland sat up till very late that night thinking of the chain of events which were now more than the imaginings of one person or two. Quinlan was his antithesis, his opposite and antidote, and yet the plain, good-hearted man had *seen*. The possibility of this being some ill-mannered joke was quite implausible. Aside from any other objections, people don't play that kind of joke on a deputy sheriff, even if the town physician is less immune. No, there was something out there . . . somebody. He was a man, or had been once, for he looked it and he wore clothes.

There were, Holland was well aware, cases of improper diagnosis. Persons have been declared dead who were not dead. There are diseases and conditions and states which resemble death and yet are not. The catatonic is one, for instance, and yet beneath his reasoning, beyond his speculating and his attempts to lay out at least in his own mind each possibility, and then rationally to plug these loopholes, he was certain as a physician that the man he had seen, the one Jamie had—so aptly wasn't it—called Mr. Mole, was not of the living.

He wished Helen were here for she was not only a good

listener—and he needed such to parade his facts and suppositions before—but she had good suggestions. The night insects were quiet and there was a hint of light in the east when the physician retired to his room.

To explain to Jamie that he was not supposed to run small-boxlike far and wide across the meadows necessitated the thinking up of a story about Indians on the move outside.

The little boy looked at his father closely, more wisely, the physician thought, than a child of his years should.

Holland went about his business glad that the days were six, five, four, then three until wife Helen would return. He could not in all conscience restrict his son to the house for there had to be a reason more than make-believe Indians and the danger to the small, tow-headed boy was not proven, dwelling perhaps more in a father's mind than anywhere else.

As the days passed, the physician chided himself a bit. He became annoyed at the feeling of uncomfortableness that he experienced when he needs be, got the coupe with the physicians' emblem over the back license plate, out of the garage to go on some necessary call or errand, and yet still felt uneasiness at leaving Jamie.

But the very passing of time gave strength to the hope that grew almost to conviction that whoever it was, whatever it was out there in the ground, moving like a mole from place to place, had gone back to whatever place from whence it had come, or had been stilled forever in some dark crave e beneath the earth's surface away from men's eyes.

Holland met Quinlan one day down in the village, and both men's spirits were good.

They didn't say so, but the meaning was clear. *I* haven't seen him nor have you or we would have spoken of it. The knowledge was between the two men and then they parted cheerfully.

The night before the good day Helen was to return, Holland's phone rang. Jamie was already upstairs, presumably asleep in his cheerful, wallpapered east room, and Holland had long since given Amanda a lift home explaining to her carefully that they'd "want her later on the morrow" because Helen would be coming back in time for supper and it would be nice to have something extra-special for her homecoming.

"Hello, Doc," it was Quinlan when Holland picked up the receiver. "Eddie's seen him again!"

The doctor's hand tightened on the instrument.

"Out back in the woods a piece. Swears he moves around an' talks to him. Wanted Eddie to take a walk with him."

Holland tried to keep his voice even: "What's to do about it, Ed?"

"Tomorrow . . ." Quinlan added just as though he'd thought it out, ". . . I'll get a bunch of us together and we'll find out who or what this is! Maybe it's some kind of queer drunk." This last, hopefully.

"I think we out to do something, Ed," the physician said resolutely. "Can't let this go on, you know!"

On that note the two men hung up, Holland to re-enter the library where he sat, the uneasiness with him again. In the last few days he had found the time and opportunity to peruse both the county clerk's and newspaper records. There had been no unaccounted-for disappearances or other incidents in this area which would explain this peripatetic "thing" which haunted the summer countryside. And in present-day society the hardest thing in the world to do is to disappear or get oneself killed or destroyed in any way without attracting considerable attention.

Yes, whoever heard of an unclaimed body or corpse? Try as he would, Holland could not dissuade himself from the nagging thought that here was something that did not fit in with the commonplace and, therefore, did not follow everyday laws of the workaday world.

Actually, it was a few minutes past seven the next morning when Holland heard his front-door knocker clattering. It seemed much earlier. The rain and mist across the land had held up the day. Jamie was just stirring in his room as his father clumped down the stairs muttering under his breath.

And then before he put his hand on the great knob that would turn the door to open it, a feeling of presentiment took hold of him, stiffened his arm and touched his back with damp, cold fingers.

He pulled the portal open, and out of the early morning grayness stepped Quinlan, in his arms a bundle, his but face wide-eyed, storm-streaked. He seemed to offer the thing cradled in his arms to Holland and Holland, seeing, suddenly became the physician.

He said gently, "Here, Ed. Let me take him," though he knew at first look it was no good.

There was dirt all over little Eddie; dirt turned to mud by the rain in his eyes and mouth and ears. The youngster had died, it was apparent, of suffocation—not from hands wrapped around his throat, but from going down deep, deep into the earth and being buried there.

The thought came back to Holland of what Quinlan had said over the phone the previous night, what his own son had said the last time the "thing" had visited over here—what was it?—Mr. Mole had invited him to take a walk *below?*

As the physician was thinking, Quinlan was talking brokenly, trying to hold onto himself with the will of a strong man, twisted and bending under the cruelest tragedy of his life.

"I'm sure the youngster was to bed when I talked to you last night, Doc, but sometime in the night or early this morning, he must have gone out—God knows why—'cept that that devil has a power, a kind of fascination! I'm up early, you know, and Eddie was nowhere around the house this morning. I went out to look . . . and there was one of those holes not far from the house. You know . . . like we'd seen before. Seen little Eddie's footprints, I did, around this place like they went into the hole. . . .

". . . I got me a spade then, Doc, and I dug faster than a man's ever dug before . . . and after I got down a ways in that hole . . . I found him . . . like this. But there weren't a 'hello, Daddy' or a breath left in 'im at all. . . ."

Quinlan sank down on a chair, sobbing now, his head between his great, strong hands, shaking like a terrified child.

"Ed," said Holland quietly, and sympathetically. "Ed, follow me into the medical room."

The physician led the way, carrying Eddie's body in his arms, and Quinlan dutifully lurched along behind. Jamie was a sensitive boy. Holland could find no use for having him look down the stairs through the bannisters and see the scene in the front hall. Also, Quinlan himself needed some medication.

The doctor laid Eddie's body carefully on the examining table, made sure with his stethoscope what he already knew—that there was not the slightest flicker of life left in the earth-choked body, and then mixed the unfortunate boy's father a potent sedative.

"He's gone, isn't he, Doc?"

"I'm afraid he is, Ed. It's a terrible thing . . . terrible! And I know any words of sympathy now from me seem poor and inadequate."

Quinlan sat for a time, not saying anything, turning the glass that contained the sedative around and around in his strong fingers. He drained the medicine, and after a while, stood up.

"Well . . . thanks, Doc. I'll take my son, if you please. Take him home and then down to the undertaker's. I want to go quick, Doc . . . 'cause I'm going to get after the devil out there in the ground! I'm going to get the men together. You'll join us, Doc?"

"You know I will, Ed. I'll come over to your place a little later in the morning."

"You got an axe, Doc? Bring it!" The deputy's teeth bared in a snarl. "We're gonna get this fellow!"

"Ed . . . don't you want me to go with you, or take little Eddie down to town myself?"

Quinlan shook his head determinedly, "What's done's done, Doc. Now we gotta get after the one who did this!"

He went out with Eddie again cradled in his arms, and the growing morning, as the light of it touched his face, showed it set in hard lines, the terrible sadness, shock and despair replaced with something else that was healthier in man.

Holland went for Jamie then and was steeled when the boy asked, "Daddy, what was Mister Quinlan doing here?"

"He had a very great problem, son," the physician replied carefully. "He came to ask me about it. How about driving into town with me, Jamie, to pick up Amanda?"

As they drove, the cloud scurried away before them and the sun came out to dry and heat up the wet, early morning world. Holland drove numbly and instinctively. He returned Amanda's greetings automatically. There was nothing to be said, but already, his son was looking at him curiously.

That was one of the curses of imagination. Amanda was old, good to bake cakes and make apple pie dumplings and filled with the desire to serve them and affection for them as a family, but she was too old to understand if he said, "Now look Amanda. Something terrible has happened in this neighborhood. There's a man loose . . . a dead man, and he's just killed a little boy. We have to be careful . . . we don't know from what direction danger may come. Maybe it won't come but there's the situation!"

He couldn't talk like that to her, or even if he could, not in front of his son.

They arrived back at the Holland house, and Amanda noticed at once that the physician had not gotten any breakfast. She insisted on getting something together. Holland ate poorly. Afterward, he must get over to Quinlan's as he had promised. The men would be gathering there for their grim task.

Jamie, from behind his glass of milk, said to his father behind his coffee cup, "I'm going over to play with Eddie this morning. We're going to fly the new kite, Daddy!"

Albert Holland swallowed with difficulty.

"No, Jamie, not this morning."

"But, Daddy—!"

What could he say? *What could he say?* Not "Jamie, I have something to tell you . . . Amanda's too old and you're really too young to understand the why of this, but the facts are, Eddie is . . . dead! He was pulled into a hole by a corpse and suffocated out there in the meadow where you and he have played so many times . . . where you were going to play this morning with your kite. He's dead, Jamie. No use looking for him out there."

How could he say that? What could he say? And all the time Jamie sitting there, tow-headed and wondering why.

"Daddy, we're going to . . ."

The boy's quick mind kept searching around his father's silence.

"Is he sick?"

(That's a doctor's son for you.)

"That's what it is!" Said the little boy, gathering momentum and sureness. "He's got measles!"

No, Jamie, that happened last winter and you don't get them twice, but you still remember how Helen and I wouldn't let you go over because Eddie had measles. This time, Jamie, it's something worse . . . oh, so much worse than measles.

"It's something catching, Daddy? Measles?"

"No."

No, Jamie not measles, not something catching—not really. Or maybe it is! Maybe that's why I'm more frightened than I'd ever dare let you know. That's why in a moment I'm going to get the axe out of the woodshed and go over and join Quinlan and the rest of the men.

Instead he said, "No, Jamie, you can't go over this morning. Find something to do around here. And don't you disobey me! I'm going to tell Amanda to keep her eye on you, hear?"

Albert Holland walked towards Quinlan's, the axe in one hand, across the low stone wall into the meadow and towards the hillside. The sun was out now, accentuating the softness and the peace of mid-summer. The fertile greenness soothed his eyes and made the unpleasant thoughts in the physician's mind seem incredible and implausible. That these things could have happened under the blueness of the sky, the brightness of the sun here in the softness of the land was surely not possible.

And yet as he walked further, he saw the knots of men standing around Quinlan's house. From a distance they were short men and tall men, fat and lean. Here and there the sun touched a gun barrel. He recognized faces as he came closer— a drugstore clerk, several boys from the volunteer fire department, the assistant postmaster, others. They nodded to him and he nodded back. And there was one thing they all had in common, and that one thing was grim and unsmiling.

Men made suggestions and barked orders at one another, and finally they walked out onto the broad bosom of the meadow taking their shovels and axes and clubs and guns with them, prodding at the earth, poking at it as though it, itself, had committed this awful crime.

Quinlan was everywhere, filled with a terrible rage that was the worse because it was silent except as it came out in the man's unquenchable energy.

The hours passed, and the men plodded across the fields, sloshed through brooks and tramped through underbrush. They had long since poked and spaded into the holes Quinlan and Dr. Holland knew of. Midday passed and afternoon. The sun slid towards the rim of the westerly hills, and Holland, consulting his watch, knew he should be getting back to get things ready for Helen.

With the fatigue of walking, searching, there came a feeling of futility. What had they done . . . what could they do? What did the know, tapping their boots and steel instruments against the ground here and there for something that would not stand up fairly and say "Here I am!"

In relays some of the men came back to Quinlan's cottage where womenfolk were keeping coffee pots on the stove. Holland left his axe at Quinlan's and turned his steps towards home. He told himself that sooner or later they'd have to uncover this creature—whatever *he* was or *it* was. It was good, he thought with a physician's analysis, that Quinlan had the direction of this posse on his hands at this moment of his so-great sorrow.

He made the house, went inside, the screen door slamming behind him. The noise of Amanda in the kitchen drew him there. She was "making something special" for the supper when Helen would be with them again.

"Where's Jamie?" He asked loudly.

Amanda was a little on the deaf side and had to be bellowed at.

"He's around—playing in his cowboy costume, he is." She waved an old arm in a semi-circle. "Doctor Albert—" she always called him that—"Doctor Albert, you look a fright! Whatever have you been doing?"

Holland looked down at himself. Five or six hours of walking through thickets and looking at dirt holes in the fields had left him rather bedraggled. He'd have to clean up. The physician looked out the window.

"Where did you say Jamie was?"

"Round somewhere," she repeated again. "Saw him not very long ago. Well, now maybe it *was* an hour. Had a friend, he did. Mister Somebody-or-other come to see him."

Holland froze. "Mister . . . Mister *Mole?*" His voice was much louder than necessary.

"That's it! Knew it sounded like an animal. Peculiar handle, isn't it, Doctor Albert? Said his friend invited him—this Mister Mole—to take a walk down below. Must mean towards the meadow, Doctor Albert."

But Holland was gone, flinging himself out the door, running and trying to look in all directions, the inner hand clamped over his heart tightening, agonizing . . .

The house was behind and the lawn and the stone wall, and then in the woods in the other direction from the meadow, he found it. A new hole like all those others!

Holland went at it with his boots and hands, wishing he had something else, but there was no time to run back for a tool. He scooped and kicked the earth away as fast as he could. And by and by a corner of material showed and then he had it in his earth-coated shaking hands. It was a hat—a small boy's cowboy hat . . . from Jamie's outfit!

The doctor redoubled his efforts then frantically, clawing, getting down on all fours, and finally he found what he knew was there, and shaking away the earth covering and clinging, he laid it on the rim of the hole he had excavated with his hands . . . the same size bundle as Quinlan had brought to him the night before, equally lifeless and useless now.

Holland made a noise like an animal, and like that animal, he dug on, hollowing and scooping, for it was for him to do this thing. *He* would have to stop it. The old who had forgotten how to dream and who don't want to believe, like Amanda, and the very young who still believe in everything, like Jamie—they had caused this, unknowing.

He went on and on, a man in an earthen hole in the green countryside. And it must have been hours later that Amanda, wondering, came looking and heard the noises from that place in the woods. She got men from the posse over at Quinlan's, and they found him like that in an unbelievably deep hole of his own making, with the small earth-caked body of his son lying guard above. It was Quinlan himself, who pulled Albert Holland out, and later with Helen, who had arrived home again, tried to reassure and quiet the physician. Helen, whose shock, at finding this terrible tragedy in her own family, was only slightly more than the frightening condition of her husband.

For Dr. Holland was not a man of science any more, nor a physician but a squealing, screaming, crying creature, stuffed with earth that came out of him when he talked. They sent for another doctor up at the county seat to come quickly, but there were miles in between, and meanwhile Holland had the time to tell over and over again how they shouldn't have pulled him out of the hole in the earth, for twice, three times, *more,* he had caught up with Mr. Mole down there. He had felt a trousered leg, an arm, a torso, and it had wriggled and twisted away from him like a worm in the earth.

Yes—and it had leered at him!

"It speaks and it moves!" Holland ranted this over and over.

Sometimes in his horror he screamed so loudly that he frightened the birds outside in the twilight of the July evening, and even poor, old half-deaf Amanda far away in other parts of the house staying, with her kindly tear-streaked face, because "Maybe there's something I can do," would clap her withered hands to her ears to keep the awful sounds from them.

But Albert Holland's screams did not carry far enough, for later, not too much later, across the green land cooling in evening, a blond child named Janice ran across the spongy green ground—a child who believed in fairy stories, in everything—running and calling through the evening, filled to bursting with the secret as she ran.

"Mommy! Daddy! Guess what! Guess what *I've* found!"

Weird Tales from Peru

Darrell Schweitzer

CLEMENTE PALMA. *Malevolent Tales.* N.p.: Strange Ports Press, 2023. Translated by Shawn Garrett. 173 pp. $23.24 hc. ISBN: 9798987681039. $16.24 tpb. ISBN: 9798987681008.
CLEMENTE PALMA. *Malignant Stories.* N.p.: Strange Ports Press, 2023. Translated by Shawn Garrett. 158 pp. $23.24 hc. ISBN: 9798987681046. $16.24 tpb. ISBN: 9798987681015.

Clemente Palma (1872–1946) was a Peruvian author who, according to the write-up on the publisher's website, was one of the first Peruvian advocates of modernism, and whose two collections (first published in 1904 and 1925) show the influence of the French Decadents and of Villers de l'Isle-Adam, he of "The Torture by Hope" fame. His work also certainly shows an awareness of Poe (unsurprising), Camille Flammarion, and Chamisso's *Peter Schlemihl* (a.k.a. *The Shadowless Man*).

While I am not able to say with any authority how Palma ranks among Peruvian authors, or how Peruvian literature figures in the larger body of South American or Spanish literature, I can describe what we English-language readers get as Palma is added to the canon of known weird literature.

I am afraid he's a fairly minor figure. While these translations are an admirable effort, they do not present us with a new Borges, much less a new Lovecraft, Machen, or Poe. Palma is an occasionally interesting writer, but no genius. Many of his stories are no more than short squibs. The very worst is "The Last Blonde," in *Malevolent Tales,* a synoptic, racist shaggy dog story fully as bad as Lovecraft's "The Street." It seems the vile, ugly Oriental race has taken over the planet and miscegenated everybody else into oblivion. Meanwhile the world's supply of gold has disappeared. The narrator has learned an alchemical recipe for gold and hopes to make himself rich by it, but is lacking the key ingredient, a lock of blonde hair. He thinks he has found the last blonde woman in the world and courts her solely for her hair, which, alas, turns out to be dyed. Yes, that is a spoiler. You are not missing anything. There are also occasional hints that Palma is none too fond of Jews, but, wisely, the publishers have decided to publish his work warts and all, rather than clean him up to the tastes of readers a century in his future.

Much better is the novelette "The Tragic Day," which is end-of-the-world science fiction, based on the notion, commonplace at the time, that when the Earth passed through the tail of Halley's Comet in 1910 all life would be snuffed out by some mysterious, lethal gas. One thinks of Wells's *In the Days of the Comet* or Conan Doyle's "The Poison Belt" (which is about poisonous "ether," not a comet, but pretty much the same thing), or Flammarion's *Omega: The Last Days of the World* (French, 1893; English, 1894). While Palma manages to sustain some narrative interest, even suspense as his characters prepare for the worst, the story is nowhere near as good as its famous exemplars, and has an ending that may will read as a copout, despite the final, cynical flourish. Some of the details ring false. I am left wondering how a house in Lima could have a Roman foundation. Palma does often set his stories in Europe and in this case it seems he forgot.

Another long one is "Mors ex Vita (Death from Life)" (in *Malignant Stories*), which is a fairly conventional tale of spiritualism and obsessive love that actually does manage to deliver a grim shock at the end. I won't spoil that one for you. Palma's other specialties are stories of cruelty and blasphemy, which were no doubt intended to scandalize his audience at the time. "Baskets" (in *Malevolent Tales*) tells how a wagon-driver carries a load of baskets containing fish over a precarious bridge. The load is not secured properly and one by one the baskets fall into the river below without the deaf driver realizing what is happening. The narrator, following behind, observes this but deliberately waits until almost all the baskets are gone and the waggoneer is financially ruined before bringing it to his attention. His reason? Because a large act of cruelty is more memorable than a small act of kindness (as would have been the case if he'd warned the man after the first basket fell). "Idealism" (in *Malevolent Tales*) suggests that love is toxic, so it is better to let the beloved die. Very depraved and decadent, but not much of a story.

"The Last Faun" (*Malevolent Tales*) suggests some of the stories of Anatole France about paganism fading before Christianity, but is, again, not as good. The last faun, with the aid of an octopus (!), seizes a young nun while she is bathing in the ocean. Voyagers nearby witness the struggle and think it's a shark attacking something, and shoot, killing both faun and nun.

Moving more directly into blasphemy, we have "Parable" (*Malevolent Tales*), in which a hermit begs Jesus to free the world of disease, want, and hatred. He does so, and life becomes so bland that humankind wants the old ways back. Goodness has no value if not achieved through struggle. Likewise in "The Fifth Gospel," Satan visits Christ on the cross and explains to him that his mission is futile. Humans prefer wickedness. They don't want to be redeemed.

Some of the outright horror stories aren't bad. "The White Farm" is about a man who is married to a dead woman for two years. They live an illusion, which is broken with tragic results. "The Vampires" (*Malevolent Tales*) suggests that the blood-sucking fiends are not the undead at all, but the psychic projections of jealous or desirous women. A young man's life is wasting away. The solution: marry the girl. This is at least an example of a vampire story outside the *Dracula* tradition.

Malignant Stories has another of Palma's blasphemies. "The Cigarette Man" is actually Satan, whose temptations are out of date. He encounters a would-be suicide and does his best to distract the fellow with wealth, youth, etc.—the usual stuff—only to be defeated by philosophical argument that mankind can already obtain anything the Devil has to offer. In the end it is Satan who hangs himself, not the narrator, and he leaves half the rope for similar use by God. "The Walpurgis" offers a vivid description of witches gathering on Walpurgis Night, although, strangely, Palma seems to think this occurs on the 30th of March, not April. "The Adventure of the Man Who Was Never Born" tells of a doppelgänger. It is the narrator, who concludes that he is the duplicate and his other self is the original.

To conclude: These stories make for an interesting exploration of macabre fiction from a slightly different cultural perspective, from a previously unfamiliar author. This is all to the good. It has to be admitted, though, that few of them rise to the highest levels of the field.

About the Contributors

Martin Andersson teaches Swedish and English at the high-school level in Gothenburg, Sweden. He coedited Lord Dunsany's *The Ghost in the Corner and Other Stories* (Hippocampus Press, 2017) with S. T. Joshi and has most recently proofread much correspondence by H. P. Lovecraft for publication.

Ramsey Campbell is an English horror fiction writer, editor, and critic who has been writing for well over fifty years. He is frequently cited as one of the leading writers in the field. His website is www.ramseycampbell.com.

Tony Fonseca is the library director at Elms College, in Chicopee, Massachusetts. He has published (under the name Anthony J. Fonseca) several books and articles on horror and dark literature, horror film, academic librarianship, musical film, and hip hop/rap music, and he co-owns the independent studio Dapper Kitty Music, which specializes in indie and meditative music.

From 1943 to 1951 *Weird Tales* published thirty-six stories by **Allison V. Harding.** It is now believed that Allison V. Harding was a pseudonym used by Jean Milligan (1919–2004) and Charles Lamont Buchanan (1919–2015) as evidenced by the work of Terence E. Hanley and *Tellers of Weird Tales.*

Alex Houstoun is a co-editor of *Dead Reckonings*. He has published *Copyright Questions and the Stories of H. P. Lovecraft,* available by contacting him at deadreckoningsjournal@gmail.com.

S. T. Joshi is a widely published literary and cultural critic and the author of *The Weird Tale* (1990), *I Am Providence: The Life and Times of H. P. Lovecraft* (2010), *Unutterable Horror: A History of Supernatural Fiction* (2012), and many other volumes. He has edited the work of H. P. Lovecraft, Ambrose Bierce, Lord Dunsany, H. L. Mencken, Leslie Stephen, and other writers.

Katherine Kerestman is the author of *Lethal* (PsychoToxin Press, 2023) and *Creepy Cat's Macabre Travels: Prowling around Haunted Towers, Crumbling Castles, and Ghoulish Graveyards* (WordCrafts Press, 2020), as well as the coeditor (with S. T. Joshi) of *The Weird Cat*, an anthology of weird cat stories by writers living and dead (WordCrafts Press, 2023). Her Lovecraftian and Gothic works have been featured in *Black Wings VII*, *Penumbra*, *Journ-E*, *Spectral Realms*, *Illumen*, *Retro-Fan*, *The Little Book of Cursed Dolls* (Media Macabre, 2023), as well as other discerning publications.

Karen Joan Kohoutek, an independent scholar and poet, has published about weird fiction in various journals and literary websites. Recent and upcoming publications have been on subjects including the Gamera films, the Robert E. Howard–H. P. Lovecraft correspondence, folk magic in the novels of Ishmael Reed, and the proto-Gothic writer Charles Brockden Brown. She lives in Fargo, North Dakota.

Michael D. Miller is a former professor of genre studies, currently writing reviews, articles, and poetry for the weird fiction genre with work appearing in *Dead Reckonings, Lovecraft Annual, Spectral Realms, Penumbra, Alien Buddha Press, Dumpster Fire Press,* and *Marchxness*. He is the author of the Realms of Fantasy RPG for Mythopoeia Games Publications.

David Peak is the author of *The World Below* (Apocalypse Party), *Eyes in the Dust and Other Stories* (Trepidatio Publishing), *Corpsepaint* (Word Horde), and *The Spectacle of the Void* (Schism). Other writing has appeared or is forthcoming in *Looming Low Volume II* (Dim Shores), *Year's Best Weird Fiction Volume Five* (Undertow Publications), *Nox Pareidolia* (Nightscape Press), *Diseases of the Head* (Punctum Books), and *Vastarien*. He lives in Baltimore by way of Chicago and New York City.

Daniel Pietersen is the editor of *I Am Stone: The Gothic Weird Tales of R. Murray Gilchrist*, part of the British Library's Tales of the Weird series. He's also a regular contributor to publications such as *Revenant* and *Horror Homeroom,* as well as a guest lecturer for the Romancing the Gothic project.

Géza A. G. Reilly is a writer and critic with an interest in twentieth-century American genre literature. A Canadian expatriate, he now lives in the wilds of Florida with his wife, Andrea, and their cat, Mim.

Darrell Schweitzer has been publishing weird or fantastic poetry for decades. Not counting comic verse, two previous collections of (mostly weird) verse are *Groping Toward the Light* (2000) and *Ghosts of Past and Future* (2008). *Dancing Before Azathoth*, a volume of previously and selected poems, is forthcoming from Hippocampus Press. His most recent story collection is *The Children of Chorazin* (Hippocampus Press, 2023) and his most recent anthology is *Shadows out of Time* (PS Publishing, 2023).

Joe Shea (The joey Zone) is an artist and illustrator. Samples of his work can be found at www.joeyzoneillustration.com.

Donald Sidney-Fryer is a poet, historian, entertainer, and one of the foremost experts on the work of Clark Ashton Smith. His latest book, *Etc. atque Etc.,* is forthcoming from Hippocampus Press.

Clint Smith is the author of the collection *The Skeleton Melodies* (Hippocampus Press, 2020), and the novella *When It's Time for Dead Things to Die* (Unnerving, 2019). Of late, his work has appeared in *American Cannibal* (Maenad Press) and *Vastarien: A Literary Journal* (Grimscribe Press).